Alain Mabanckou was born in 1966 in Congo. An award-winning novelist, poet and essayist, Mabanckou currently lives in Los Angeles, where he teaches literature at UCLA. His six novels *African Psycho*, *Memoirs of a Porcupine*, *Broken Glass*, *Black Bazaar*, *Tomorrow I'll Be Twenty* – a fictionalised retelling of Mabanckou's childhood in Congo – and his most recent, *Black Moses*, are all published by Serpent's Tail. Among his many honours are the Prix Renaudot for *Memoirs of a Porcupine*, a Prix Goncourt shortlisting for *Black Moses*, and the Académie Française's Grand prix de littérature, awarded in recognition of his entire literary career. His memoir *The Lights of Pointe-Noire* won the 2016 French Voices Award and was described by Salman Rushdie as 'a beautiful book'. He is a Chevalier of the Légion d'honneur and an officer of the Ordre des Arts et des Lettres, was a finalist for the 2015 Man Booker International Prize and has featured on *Vanity Fair*'s list of France's fifty most influential people.

Praise for *African Psycho*

'A morbid parody of the serial-killer genre that owes as much to Albert Camus's *The Outsider* as to Bret Easton Ellis ... insisting on laughter in the midst of desperation, [Mabanckou] sugars the pill of criticism with humour that veers from the gently ironic to the bawdy or macabre' *Economist*

'This is *Taxi Driver* for Africa's blank generation ... a deftly ironic Grand Guignol, a pulp fiction vision of Frantz Fanon's *The Wretched of the Earth* that somehow manages to be both frightening and self-mocking at the same time' *Time Out*, New York

'A macabre ' er' *Vanity Fair*

'A smart satire on the deserving targets of corrupt official-dom, complacent media and blank-eyed consumerism' *New Internationalist*

'Mabanckou manages to write playfully about an alarming subject' *Financial Times*

'Energetic, terrifically powerful writing' Harriett Gilbert, BBC Radio 4's *A Good Read*

Praise for Alain Mabanckou

'Alain Mabanckou addresses the reader with exuberant inventiveness in novels that are brilliantly imaginative in their forms of storytelling. His voice is vividly colloquial, mischievous and often outrageous as he explores, from multiple angles, the country where he grew up, drawing on its political conflicts and compromises, disappointments and hopes. He acts the jester, but with serious intent and lacerating effect' Man Booker International Prize judges' citation

'A dizzying combination of erudition, bawdy humour and linguistic effervescence' *Financial Times*

'A hugely engaging storyteller whose humour, mischief and sheer bravura only throw the melancholy of his forlorn migrant heroes into even bolder relief ... Mabanckou conjures a world where ragged modernisation coincides with tentacular kin networks and traditional lore' *Independent*

'An inventive and playful writer' *Herald*

'Mabanckou's rhythmic and lyrical lines draw us into his characters and communities at a tempo that mirrors the speed of speech' *Australian*

AFRICAN PSYCHO

ALAIN MABANCKOU

Translated by Christine Schwartz Hartley

First published in Great Britain in 2008 by Serpent's Tail,
an imprint of Profile Books Ltd
3 Holford Yard
Bevin Way
London
WC1X 9HD
www.serpentstail.com

First published in 2003 by Le Serpent à Plumes, France
First published in this translation in 2007 by
Soft Skull Press, Brooklyn, New York

1 3 5 7 9 10 8 6 4 2

Designed and typeset by Mathew Lyons
Printed and bound by Mackays of Chatham, Kent

A CIP record for this book can be obtained from the British Library

ISBN 978 1 78125 787 6
eISBN 978 1 84765 473 1

Besides, am I truly a murderer? I have killed a human being, but it seems to me I haven't done it myself…

—Hermann Ungar, *Boys & Murderers*

My Idol and Great Master Angoualima

1.

I have decided to kill Germaine on December 29. I have been thinking about this for weeks—whatever one may say about it, killing someone requires both psychological and logistical preparedness. I believe I have now reached the necessary state of mind, even if I have yet to choose the means by which I will do the deed. It is now a question of detail. I'd rather give myself a bit of latitude on this practical point, and in so doing add a measure of improvisation to my project.

I am not looking for perfection, no—far be it from me. As a matter of fact, I do not like to undertake anything without due consideration, and a murder is not going to change the way I go about doing things…

Reading news items in our town's dailies, I find that no gesture is as simple as that of bringing someone's life to an end. All you need to do is procure a weapon, whatever it may be, set a trap for the future victim and, finally, proceed. The police and the courts will then get on with their job, trying to figure out the murderer's motives. These keepers of the law will even go so far as to credit a scoundrel with genius when in fact his deed was so absolutely logical that it needed no such speculation. But the poor bastards have to work, don't they? This is what they get paid for, and to some extent it is thanks to people like us that they earn a living. I wonder what they will say about me once I have committed my crime. The worst would be that it goes unnoticed. Of course I am not about to consider this humiliating possibility. Why then would I have spent days in deep reflection, during which my brain got all tangled up, trying to choose the right weapon for this upcoming crime—so much so that I practically found myself on the verge of a nervous breakdown?

Ideally, I would enjoy as much media coverage as my idol, Angoualima, the most famous of our country's assassins. From time to time, to give thanks for his genius, to keep him informed of what I am doing, or even just for the pleasure of talking to him, I make my way to the cemetery of the Dead-Who-Are-Not-Allowed-To-Sleep and kneel in front of his grave. And there, as if by magic, I swear, the Great Master of crime appears before me, as charismatic as in his glory days. We converse in the privacy of this sinister locale, the haunt of crows and other birds of bad omen...

I refrain from dreaming.

Angoualima had intuition, crime and highway robbery fit him like a glove. Can you imagine someone who was born with one extra finger on each hand? Not the type of additional little fingers you notice on some individuals, which surgery can fix with success. Those were real fingers, as necessary as the other ten, and he could really move them around. He would use them to scratch his body's hard-to-reach places, no doubt, and to satisfy his criminal impulses as well. I myself do not have such additional fingers, I know. I am not going to make a big deal out of it.

In fact our view, which we find comforting, is that the assassin should possess something more than those things possessed by your ordinary human being. On this subject, I will soon reveal the reasons why, to this day, I am disgusted by the speeches delivered by our city's public prosecutors. Taking advantage of the fact that, in contrast to the other, "seated" magistrates, they are perched up in one corner of the room, where the public necessarily notices them, they seem to believe that they are entitled to lecture the accused. This goes to their heads, and they launch into rhetorical flourishes that make them look like the most intelligent people in court. You really have to see these people, their robes, and the way they swish their ample sleeves around, a move they must surely practice in front of the mirror, expecting their wives' approving gazes.

In the time when I was still hanging around our city's courts, I found our prosecutors had a pretty fucking high opinion of themselves. They thought they were celebrities, showing up last in the courtroom with the excuse that they had forgotten a file that was important for the continuation of the case of the day. Then they would assume serious airs and wait until the presiding judge called on them to speak, to start performing one of their trademark coquettish numbers for us...

Nothing about me would be of any interest to those who believe one is born a criminal. Such theories are a lot of nonsense, I say! And what else, now? To think that people spend their lives studying, analyzing all this from up close! Don't they have anything else to do? When criminals, real ones, start teaching their subject themselves, then I will begin to believe such things. Most of the time, though, we're bored to tears by eggheads with no criminal practice of their own, reciting things they have learned in books written by people who are liars, as they are themselves!

Let me make things clear: I do not wish to become bigger than Angoualima or graft little fingers onto my hands. I want to be appreciated in proportion to the result of my criminal gesture. Being unable to match the Great Master's feats, I would at least like to be considered his spiritual heir. To achieve this, I know I have some more work to do: killing Germaine on December 29—that is, two days from today—is only one step toward my coronation…

2.

I still cannot understand why my last deed, which took place only three months ago, wasn't covered by the national press or the press of the country over there. Only four insignificant lines in The Street Is Dying, a small neighbor-hood weekly, and the lines devoted to my crime were buried between ads for Monganga soap and No-Confidence shoes. As I have kept the clipping, I can't help laughing when I read it again:

> *A nurse at Adolphe-Cissé Hospital was assaulted by a sex maniac upon her return home from work. A complaint was filed at the police station of the He-Who-Drinks-Water-Is-An-Idiot neighborhood.*

I assure you, I spent the whole day after this deed listening to Radio Right Bank in the hope that it would convey the facts in detail to make up for this short news item, which, even though I wasn't named in it, had hurt my pride and come as a real snub to me—I have always suffered from the fact that my actions keep being credited to some other of the town's shady characters.

But they said nothing! This was the day I understood the meaning of radio silence. I became aware that my gesture was not worthy of a criminal of Angoualima's ilk, he who would leave his mark by sending his victims' private parts to the national press and to the press of the country over there by registered mail.

I'm telling you: Angoualima, my idol, was something else. How could I not think about him? I make no secret of the fact that his disappearance upset me a great deal at the time, although it did help the police who had been looking for him for years. It just wasn't possible that the Great Master would die like this, as if he didn't have any personality, and that he would leave me an orphan. Seeing the man who used to put the city to fire and sword now immobile, his body left to the winds blowing in from the sea, in the center of a circle he had drawn himself— who would have believed it? I was abandoned. I no longer had reason to live. I cried. I resented the authorities and the inhabitants of He-Who-Drinks-Water-Is-An-Idiot. People here and there expressed relief, but I cried foul. Surely, my idol had been pushed to the limit. By way of consolation, I told myself that this death was an opportunity for me. Having never come into contact with the Great Master when he was alive, I now had the opportunity to pay him a visit, at his gravesite. His spirit would talk to me...

The entire city knows that before committing suicide, my idol, Angoualima, had sent the national press and the press of the country over there an audio tape on which he spent 120 minutes repeating, "I shit on society," the very words that the neighborhood's most popular band, the Brothers The-Same-People-Always-Get-To-Eat-In-This-Shitty-Country, later used in their hit song.

It's true his end came as a surprise to everyone. No one could have thought of it. Here was my idol, thumbing his nose one last time. He'd really shat on society, as he said. I now understand what he was doing: above all, he wanted to avoid entering legend on his knees, like a boxer, long at the top of his game, who's humiliated by some unknown challenger just as his career is waning.

In this sense, then, the Great Master had known how to leave the ring before having to face one fight too many. That's how I choose to interpret his venerable gesture. I'm not interested in what was discussed later...

Still, it's weird: every time one of my deeds ends in fiasco, something—I don't know what exactly—compels me to think about Angoualima, my idol, and, in the first hours of the day, to make for his grave in the cemetery of The-Dead-Who-Are-Not-Allowed-To-Sleep. There I talk to him, listen to him take me to task, call me an imbecile, an idiot, or a pathetic character. I agree, abandon myself to the fascination he exerts over me, and take these insults as a sign of the affection that only he shows me. Now if only I could convince myself that it is not in my interest to compare myself to him or desperately seek his approval as a master of crime, I might be able to start working with a free spirit. To each his own manner and personality. I certainly have tried to pursue this course. It's not as simple as it seems.

Why take Angoualima as a model and not another of our town's bandits? I finally found an explanation. Actually, back when I was a mere teenager with skeletal legs, drifting through the sticky streets of the He-Who-Drinks-Water-Is-An-Idiot neighbor-hood and playing rag-ball with other kids my age, I had already heard people talk about Angoualima and recognized myself in each of his gestures, which the whole country decried. I felt admiration for him. In a certain way he preceded me in the type of existence I dreamed of for myself. To fend off despair, I persuaded myself that I resembled him, that his destiny and mine had the same arc, and that little by little I would eventually climb each step until my head, shaped like a rectangular brick, deserved a crown of laurels.

I did resemble him. Not in any physical sense, but in that he also had cultivated a taste for solitude and that he hadn't been recognized by his parents either—they had abandoned him at a great crossroads of life where the poor child had no idea what path to take...

Hearing grownups talk about Angoualima's life made me realize I had not known my own parents. Just like my idol, I had fled most of the families in which the government forcefully placed me. I was called a "picked-up child," like the kids with whom I played rag-ball behind the train station of He-Who-Drinks-Water-Is-An-Idiot. I remember the red soil, broken glass and garbage the inhabitants came to dump around the field. We would be in the middle of this refuse, laughing and carefree, shirtless, running like crazy until nightfall after a ball made of rags.

We were called "picked-up children" because at the time, following an unwanted pregnancy, a great number of mothers would wait until they had delivered to skip out of the maternity ward and leave the task of caring for their progeny to the State.

I have always imagined the woman who brought me into the world running in a loincloth saturated with amniotic fluid. I don't know why I hang on to this morbid image, but if I could kill all the women on Earth, I would begin with my mother—if only someone would show her to me, even now. I would pull out her heart of stone, cook it in my shop's furnace and eat it with sweet potatoes, licking my fingers, the rest of her body rotting away in front of me...

Just like Angoualima, I loathed the thought of living with these host families who, in spite of their philanthropic impulse, viewed a "picked-up child" as they would an animal found in the street, giving it milk until its owners come get it. I would always escape from these fortresses, and God knows many welcomed me. As a matter of fact, it was during this period that I executed my first dangerous deed, this one more with the intention of defending myself than anything else, for I had my back against the wall...

I can still picture myself on that day.

I was living in the center of town, with a family of very cultivated civil servants who boasted they had chosen me after a rigorous selection process involving a hundred or so "picked-up children" because, being the one who always ran away, I obviously needed to be taken care of more than anyone else.

For one year I stayed with these well-mannered people. They would ambush me to test the level of my intelligence. Then they noted with sighs of relief that I hadn't forgotten the concepts I had learned a few days earlier. They wanted to inculcate everything in me, and in no time at all: How to behave at the table, how to respond to grownups, how to sneeze, burp or yawn, how to keep my urine stream from ringing loudly against the porcelain while I peed, how to hold my farts, at what time I was to go to bed, how to read in silence and without running my fingers under the words. They made me wear cumbersome clothes made out of old wrinkle-free nylon with silk lining, when it was more than forty degrees Celsius in the shade! The best tailor in the area would make my clothes—and what clothes! The buttons, big as coins, went up to my neck. I suffocated and sweated heavily under the sun. In their eyes, I had apparently become presentable. I no longer looked like one of those street kids with holes in their pants who stank like mangy dogs. I was distinguished and clean, a child who was lucky to get an education. Was I happy, fundamentally? Was I at ease, dressed in clothes poorly adapted to my nature as a boisterous kid?

All this would have been okay if they hadn't shaved this rectangular head of mine completely, making me prey to the jeers of the other children, who would spend all day shouting, "Baldy, baldy!"

Tears in my eyes, I ran. In my hand I held a rock, determined to throw it at the first of them to show up.

My adoptive family taught me tolerance. I was to offer the other cheek to the person who had just slapped me because this was how you did things and there was no debating God's will, especially when it was written in black and white in the Holy Book.

I was told that I would become a responsible man, a cultivated man, a fine man, because ignorance plunged human beings further into darkness whereas every concept learned brought them gradually closer to the light. I was then studious, or rather pretended to be. On certain evenings around six, with other kids, I would go to catechism, where a sister made it her business to save us from the error of our ways. Her face bore the scars of her tribe. The sternness lurking behind her gaze kept me from looking her straight in the eye. God inspired fear in me, and the paths that led to Him seemed to me tortuous indeed. I think it was worse than at school. This sister claimed she was "chasing" away our sins and opening us to the real life, the eternal life, for among God's children there were no distinctions—small, tall, fat, thin, black, white, yellow, red: God couldn't care less, she said. Yet every month we had to endure a thorough exam, first oral, then written. Down to the last detail, the sister with the scarred face would check whether we were absorbing God's Word. What surprised me was that she held a long whip and did not hesitate to smack us when our memory failed us repeatedly…

The People's School was located a few hundred meters from my adoptive parents' residence. They would drop me in front of the gate and watch me walk away with a school bag I held with the tips of my fingers. We lined up in front of the classroom and the teacher then called our names to take attendance. With the other kids making fun of my rectangular head, the teacher deemed it preferable for me to sit in the last row. Otherwise, those sitting behind me would throw paper balls that landed atop my shaved scalp…

School? I was elsewhere, even if I basically knew that with application I would be able to distinguish myself from the other students. I pretended I didn't understand anything for the mere pleasure of seeing our teacher linger over me and look at my rectangular head with indulgence. Surely he told himself that it was just an empty shell and that, for all his efforts, he couldn't make it absorb anything that wasn't there before. Me, I laughed about it on the way home—I was able to solve all these multiplications, divisions and fractions from memory, without using my fingers or little sticks made out of reed like the other students did...

I was meant to leave this good family as well, but this time around, I will always remember, it was in the most unexpected and tragic manner. At least as far as my "adoptive parents" were concerned...

I had just turned eleven. Given my unattractive appearance, you might think me three or four years older, no more. This family had an only son who was three years older than I and attended not the People's School but a private school where the children of European aid cadres would go. Yet the rogue would spend his time outside with the big kids from the working-class districts and use me as a guinea pig for experiments he picked up from the street. Once his parents were gone, and when I refused to indulge his spoiled-child whims, he would whip me to amuse himself. Despite his age, he still wet his bed frequently, and he raised his voice in front of his parents. Whenever they cited me as an example, this only son would sulk all day and resist eating and going to school. To secure a gift his parents refused to buy him, he threatened not to wash for a week and defecate in his bed. The father would capitulate and beg him on his knees...

So it was that one day he grabbed my shirt collar, pulled me into the bedroom we shared, and told me while waving a stick in the air:

"Take off your pants. We're going to do like daddies and

mommies! You're mommy and I'm daddy."

I had failed to notice that he had hidden a fake beard under one of our bunk beds. He put on the beard to look like his father and frowned his eyebrows to intimidate me.

"Hurry up before my daddy and my mommy come back! You'll see, it's good and we'll do it every day!"

He was erect like a horse under his pants and suspenders. I could not escape: he was standing in front of the door and beating the floor with his stick like bailiffs at court announcing the arrival of a judge and the beginning of a hearing.

I was trapped. The bedroom now seemed narrow and dark despite a feeble glimmer from an old bulb above our heads. I had to do something to get out of this situation. I don't know how exactly, but an ingenious idea came to me, a way I could swing things back in my favor. I had to play along, I told myself.

"You don't know how to do it!" I said, trying to taunt him.

"What? What are you saying? You crazy or what?"

"No, you don't know how to do it, that's not the way it's done."

"I do it with the big kids outside!" he replied angrily. "I'm tired of always being the mommy, today I'll be the daddy, take off your pants, quick!"

Hands in my pockets, I replied calmly:

"Usually when daddies and mommies do this, the daddies must always close their eyes when the mommies take off their clothes. And then you have to turn off the light because it's not good to see when you do that…"

"How do you know these things, huh? You do this too?" he asked, surprised and disarmed by what I had said.

"That's how my daddy and my mommy used to do it, I swear," I said while raising my right hand.

"You're lying, Baldy!"

"No, I'm not lying…"

"Yes, you're lying! My daddy and mommy told me that you're a picked-up child, and therefore you didn't see your real daddy and real mommy do that!"

"I did too!"

"When, then?" he asked, defiant, raising his stick higher.

"I was picked up, but only after my daddy and mommy died! I saw them, I swear!"

"And how did you manage to see them do it?"

"I hid under their bed."

The only son fell silent for a moment. I saw doubt seize him. Resigned and out of arguments, he lowered his stick.

"Fine," he said, "you're right, okay! I'm turning off the light, turning my back and closing my eyes. But I'm counting to five! Take off your pants or I'll whip you very very hard!"

He turned off the light. I could still make out his silhouette in the doorway. As soon as his back was turned, I grabbed the stick he used as a whip by surprise. The other end was pointy. He turned around, felt for the switch in the dark. The light came back on, more intense than before. I had only a few fractions of a second to act.

Thinking of the *Zorro* comics I stole from the bookstore-on-the-pavement outside the Duo movie theater, I attacked, holding the stick like a spear. Bull's-eye. Immediately I heard the bad boy scream. "Baldy! Baldy!" He cried for help and groped for a cloth to wipe the abundant gooey liquid that oozed from the eye I had just pierced…

I left this house and entrenched myself forever in the He-Who-Drinks-Water-Is-An-Idiot neighborhood. In the years that followed, I embarked on an adventure. I became aware that I had to fashion myself by trampling society's rules. For days and nights at a time, I would hide near the shanties by the stream that cuts our city in two. Amongst the picked-up children, I went almost unnoticed. I had to carve a place for myself, to distinguish myself. But I never begged, thank God. Despair has its limits.

So I had to keep myself busy, find an activity that allowed me at least to secure a meal every night. I ran errands for old bums who tossed me a few coins. I was deemed obliging, obedient. I didn't speak much. These old folks didn't even know my name.

I no longer returned to town like the other kids who went there to steal apples, croissants and grapes from Score, the shop that catered to our city's whites and wealthy. I disappeared from sight, sleeping wherever night caught me, and most often under the tables of our district's little markets. I was at the mercy of the street, and later on, the gangs of picked-up children who were slightly older than me adopted me because I was fearless and cold-blooded. The group fed my enthusiasm. We shared the loot even when I hadn't been in on the job. This was the solidarity of pariahs.

Little by little, I imposed myself as a leader among picked-up children. People feared me after I told the story of my "adoptive brother's" pierced eye. That was my argument to intimidate those who believed I needed to show them allegiance because they were my elders.

From then on the group applauded my plans, and I was among the leaders for every job we thought up.

I suppose my last adoptive family, about whom I haven't heard any news in ages, kept the story quiet and refused to lodge a complaint. In these rich circles from the center of town, people are serious about being discreet.

I may still resent these adoptive families, but I thank them all the same. Don't get the wrong idea. I too have emotions, like everybody else, and human behavior can sometimes move me to tears. I thank these families because they pulled me out of the darkness of ignorance a little by teaching me how to read and write—in scattered little scraps, certainly, but scraps I was later able to piece together by myself thanks to the books I stole from the bookstore-on-the-pavement, in front of the Duo movie theater. I liked the comic-strip character Blek le Roc very much, with his impressive musculature and Herculean strength. In his adventures, this hero was accompanied by two other characters: Professor Occultis and the young Roddy. The former searched ceaselessly for the philosopher's stone. He was endowed with uncommon intelligence. His heavy-set physique and elegantly trimmed mustache won me over. The young Roddy was a teenager whose face was peppered with freckles. He was the most fragile of the three heroes. Still, he managed to extricate himself from the most hopelessly entangled situations. I believed these characters were real and lived someplace where they devoted their lives to the defense of freedom, adventure and heroism. I started hating them the day I realized that there was a human being drawing them in France, that it was he who had them run throughout the world, and that their adventures were just a figment of his imagination...

Zorro and *Blek le Roc* were not the only comic strips among these books—no. I am not about to cite all those I found fascinating. I can say, however, that the ones I read allowed me to travel, to go far, to see other horizons, and sometimes—such as in *La Brute* by Guy des Cars—to find out the manner in which criminals accomplish their deeds. I mention this book because I cried at the misfortune of this poor deaf-dumb-blind character unjustly accused of having murdered his spouse with a paper-cutter during a cruise...

But wait! Don't get the wrong idea. I also threw myself into reading what people call great literature, I did. To each his own. What I was looking for, personally, was action, fear, which I found above all in pulp literature. People said, however, that in order to be an educated man, you had to immerse yourself in the likes of Proust, Genet, Céline, Rousseau and a great many others of that ilk. How could I possibly buy these books? As a matter of fact, the priests at Saint-Jean-de-Bosco church caught me stealing the prestigious titles of the Pleiade collection a number of times. They prayed for me and asked me to confess. I stopped pinching these books because, after my confession, Father Mathieu lectured me for an hour then handed me, free of charge, a copy of the book I had stolen, accompanied by a pocket Bible.

It wasn't shame I felt, but rather the irony of it all, looking at Father Mathieu, with his big glasses, bald spot and scratchy voice...

3.

There are uncertainties I would like to address right away: my eclectic upbringing in the host families and the education I received in the street forged in me a disposition that bears some resemblance to mayonnaise gone bad. So it is that I can both hold forth in a language that some would deem correct, studied, and at any moment plunge into the most shocking vulgarity, especially when I start talking to myself before or after my dangerous deeds. At this point, I can no longer stop myself—I string together remarks, sentences, without controlling myself. I know a thing or two about coarse language. It may also be sweetened by the Holy Book readings imposed on me during my youth. You think you can rebel against these things, but a few stigmata remain forever. It can't be helped…

Yes, I love vulgarity. I claim it loud and clear. I love it because only it says what we are, without the hideous masks we wear by nature, which turn us into mean beings, hypocrites, ceaselessly running after decency, a quality I couldn't care less about. I'm not the type who can control himself when someone comes after me in my territory. I'm not asking anything of anybody. All I want is peace and quiet in my native corner. Those inclined to judge me vulgar will be shown not to have understood a thing about my personality. Fundamentally, does this bother me? I have learned not to take people's opinions into account anymore…

Time really does go fast.

A good many years after the heinous crime against my adoptive brother, and despite all the temptation, I had yet to attempt crossing the Mayi River to go live in the country over there, which was said to have been on my idol Angoualima's itinerary. In truth, imagining that I had to follow the Great Master's course to the letter, I was a hair's breadth away from deciding to do just that. But it would have meant forgetting that this neighborhood, He-Who-Drinks-Water-Is-An-Idiot, is my life. It is my territory, a place I will defend until my last breath. Its honor is the reason I am fighting. Its image is dear to my heart. I know the inhabitants of this rat hole have a poor image in this country. But is it their fault? Do the inhabitants themselves sully this neighborhood? It's easy to point the finger at us, to scapegoat us and do God knows what else. The problem doesn't lie here.

I must calm down.

Still, you must understand: I don't appreciate it when people come and defile this place. My life is this sordid little patch that the authorities look upon with chagrin and visit only at election time. Yes, this is where I grew up. This is where I happily dragged my skeletal legs and rectangular head. This is where I learned the sheet-iron and auto-body trade in the shops of old folks who graciously took me in until such time as my work became respectable in the eyes of the population. I'd fix the beat-up cars of the leading citizens of He-Who-Drinks-Water-Is-An-Idiot: military men, veterans, ministers' mistresses and more.

My plot of land? Let's talk about it! I bought it with my savings, I swear, God be my witness.

My house? Please. I built it myself, albeit with the help of a mason friend. And so what? Didn't I pick up cement bags and handle a trowel by his side? That's why I always say I built my house with my own hands. Same for the shop just out back.

Do I have to stress that I have no flowery memories from my youth other than those of the soccer games with rag-balls?

Yes, I have stolen, but with fewer repercussions than my

idol, Angoualima. Was it because I heard people talk about him that I wanted to follow blindly in his tracks? I cannot answer this question. In everything he undertakes, man needs a model, a solid reference. As far as banditry and crime were concerned, who in our country could have held a candle to the Great Master Angoualima? I had no idea then, and have none still. So I bided my time, convinced that there was no rush, that someday things would happen by themselves. I could not commit astounding deeds at that time—my hands were not as large as they are today, capable of choking my potential victims. So I satisfied myself with small thefts here and there. Ambushes I set up for elderly people in the nocturnal confusion of He-Who-Drinks-Water-Is-An-Idiot's dirty alleys. I snatched their satchels or wallets and ran through the neighborhood that no longer held any secrets for me. I took the money and ripped their IDs or threw them on one of the two banks of the stream that cuts our city in two. The next morning, congratulating myself, I listened to Radio Right Bank's newsflashes announcing that this woman's ID or that old man's invalid card had been recovered…

Nevertheless, just before I came of age, there were a few audacious acts that testified to the fact that I was acquiring more and more experience, and that I was now entitled to a change in status in our city's underworld. The list of these acts is actually quite long, if I go back to the time when I associated myself with the picked-up children of He-Who-Drinks-Water-Is-An-Idiot. Some have hardly left a significant trace in my memory and there would be no justifying my dwelling on them. The ones that count for me are those I perpetrated alone, to the best of my knowledge and belief, without waiting around for a plan hatched in common, with roles divvied up according to a ringleader's wishes.

So then, from this point of view, I can say the most interesting offense in my time as a solitary bandit was without doubt the one I committed in the fancy neighborhood now called the Right Bank district by our current mayor. The victim I had chosen was Master Fernandes Quiroga, a mixed-race whose office as a notary* was located across from the Kassaï roundabout, in the center of town. This man was not just a notary; he was also active as a real estate agent. I can't begin to tell you how much confusion this engendered. In our country, holding several jobs, even the most incompatible ones, doesn't bother anyone. Fernandes Quiroga leaned on his clients, and they sold their property under pressure from him, when in fact they had originally come to him to leave this property to their descendents in a will, as is typically done. For our public servant, a notary's deed was less lucrative than a transaction conducted with his realtor's cap on.

Three reasons had led me to resent this respectable man from the center of town.

To begin with, he drove a new Mercedes with smoked windows, and I felt offended by his success, by the manner in which he showed it off to the rest of the population, which was rotting in extreme indigence. I had never touched the body or the engine of such a prestigious car.

Should a vehicle of this German make be brought to our shop, it was always my apprenticeship master who took care of it himself. He did not conceal his pride and would try the

---

* Translator's note: As an officer of the law, a notary is charged with executing authentic deeds, most commonly ensuring that sales of real estate, estate dispersals and wedding contracts are fairly and properly drafted and executed.

vehicle out, parading in front of He-Who-Drinks-Water-Is-An-Idiot's watering holes.

The second reason was the most painful one for me because it stirred my emotions and showed me that I was but mere refuse, incapable of charm. As it happened, Master Quiroga paid regular visits to one of his mistresses in He-Who-Drinks-Water-Is-An-Idiot. She was a light-skinned girl, tall, barely escaped from adolescence. Grownups said she was the most beautiful in He-Who-Drinks-Water-Is-An-Idiot, and even in our city. I don't know about that, but I had loving feelings for her, sort of, and felt something swell in my underpants whenever I caught sight of her. At the time, I masturbated four to five times a day while imagining the girl's silhouette. Might she ever set her beauty-queen gaze on my hideous, rectangular-headed person? I had no illusions on that subject. This girl lived on the other side of the district, in the area where families were not too comfortable but still ate their fill. Their plot of land was located across from where I was doing my last apprenticeship as an auto-body and sheet-iron worker. I arrived at work the moment she stepped out with a basket of woven creepers, headed for the Great Market. When she opened the fence to their plot, I stopped at the garage entrance and pretended to be looking for something in my pockets. She walked on, ignoring my presence. I stayed on, contemplating her proud bearing and the heavy bosom that made her white t-shirt ride up so you could catch a glimpse of her tiny belly button, which you couldn't miss for the ring she had hung there, I don't know how. Powerless, like a statue made of salt, I watched her disappear into the horizon. Coming to, I rushed to the shop's sheet-iron toilets. I closed the door, secured it well with three big bricks for fear my apprenticeship master would turn up unexpectedly—he never knocked. Then I lowered my overalls and started playing with my sexual organ. I held my breath to avoid letting out a growl when I emptied myself. One day, the other apprentices discovered what I was up to. Lucky for me, the boss was away. I was touching my private parts with greater fervor that day. And because it had been a few weeks since I'd played with myself, I came with the intensity of an electrical discharge. I found myself on the floor, like a cassava bag dropped by a clumsy warehouse handler. The toilets' sheet-iron plates collapsed, and my colleagues discovered me half-naked, my pubic area saturated with Monganga soap bubbles. For a long time after I was the object of their derision...

I was more or less aware of Fernandes Quiroga's mistress's schedule. She would be standing in the street toward the end of the day. Our leading citizen would park his Mercedes and eventually come out of the luxurious vehicle, well dressed, with suits like those I had seen that time at the Duo movie theater, in a film titled Les tontons flingueurs, if memory serves me correctly. With a studied gesture, Fernandes Quiroga would open the car's back door and grab a large bouquet of roses. The young girl would chirp with happiness. Meanwhile, contorted by a sudden, suffocating burst of rancor, I bit my tongue.

And so it was that one afternoon, unable to stand it anymore, I followed Master Quiroga in an old car entrusted to us for repair, which my apprenticeship master, who was also teaching me a bit of mechanics, had allowed me to try out in the neighborhood. Ordinarily, Fernandes Quiroga came to his mistress in the evening. What had gotten into him to show up in this afternoon that day? From what I could gather, he didn't find the girl at home and was beside himself. That wasn't my problem. I drove slowly. There were two cars between the notary–real estate agent's Mercedes and mine. I had transgressed my apprenticeship master's orders by wandering away from He-Who-Drinks-Water-Is-An-Idiot's alleys and going into the center of town. On that day, I was finally able to find out where Fernandes Quiroga's office was located.

When I returned to the garage, my master was livid because I'd taken too much time and he'd feared an accident. I explained to him that the car needed to be put to the test outside He-Who-Drinks-Water-Is-An-Idiot's thoroughfares…

A third reason led me to go after this notary–real estate agent: I thought he kept money in a safe in his office. This presented me the opportunity to get my hands on a hoard, a nice change from the crumbs I stole from the neighborhood's defenseless old people. Quiroga was likely to hide his savings in his study. You don't trust banks in our country. In fact, it's not unusual to arrive at a teller's window and hear him tell you that there is no money left and that you should come back tomorrow, although he cannot be certain his coffers will be replenished. As a result, the population wonders what bankers do with their clients' deposits. It is for this reason, the neighborhood's gray beards say, that it is more prudent to keep your money under the mattress or in pillowcases…

Finally one evening, after much hesitation, I decided to proceed. I took a bus and arrived in front of the building where Master Quiroga had his office, a hammer in the back pocket of my jeans. I was wearing a long beige overcoat that concealed this tool.

The building was well kept, surrounded by greenery that must have been cut every other day. There was also an immense garden with impressive fountains that rose almost as high as the building. The caretaker opened the door for me after I showed him my hammer with the broad smile of a man who knew what apartment he was going to. He thought I was a workman called in a rush by one of the tenants.

I didn't take the elevator but climbed up the stairs in the dark.

On the third floor, I took a breather for a few minutes so as to appear serene. When the light came back on, I saw a little silver plaque on one of the three doors, the middle one:

FERNANDES QUIROGA
NOTARY–REAL ESTATE AGENT

I rang, and after a moment's wait the door opened. I found myself in front of a man of about forty, of mixed race, tall, his hair cut short and parted in the middle, and with round glasses. He was wearing a white shirt with an Italian collar and a black silk tie with a knot as impeccable as that of a young colonel proud of his lightning rise through the ranks. His pants, also black with thin white stripes, showed how attached he was to wearing matching colors, even if this ensemble made him look rather like an undertaker who fancied he could brighten up his trade via sartorial means.

His eyes widened with amazement when he saw me at the door to his office. He was Master Fernandes Quiroga alright, such as I had always seen him in my neighborhood's alleys when he came to visit his mistress.

He stood in the middle of the doorway, his hands

blocking the entrance to his office.

"You are mistaken, young man," he said.

"No," I insisted. "I have come to see you."

He reminded me that his office was closed and that he saw people by appointment only.

I don't know where it came from, my sudden idea to tell him that it was urgent, that I had to talk to him about my plan to sell two plots of land that I had just inherited from my grandmother, that the entire city had praised his services and his effectiveness.

"But your parents are the ones who should be making an appointment with me, young man!"

"I don't have any parents."

"Fine, but you surely have a guardian?"

"Yes, but that was my grandmother, who just died."

He looked at me from head to toe, as if marvelling that there were still people on Earth crazy enough to will their possessions to the worst kinds of degenerates like me. Nevertheless, he beckoned me in and pointed to an armchair of the kind that rich people have in their houses, maybe one of those Louis something or other.

"The office is closed, I am about to step out, but I will listen to you for a few minutes, just for my information, and we will make an appointment to look at all this more closely. So you have just inherited two plots of land?"

"Yes," I replied, my voice calm and convincing.

"Where are they located?"

"Right here in the fancy neighborhood."

"Interesting! Interesting! And what proves you are the only heir?"

"My grandmother had only one child, my mother. My mother is already dead; she had only one child, and that's me…"

"That's all fine, but I need a written document testifying to the fact that the *decujus'* last wishes were entirely in your favor! Do you realize what would happen if someday another individual showed up here and said he is also an heir to the same plots?"

"What does *decujus* mean?" I interrupted the notary–realtor, hoping to lengthen the conversation and find the opportune moment for my deed.

"You're right, young man, forgive me: it's force of habit. Let's talk simply: the *decujus* is the deceased person. But let's come back to where we were. There could be issues of joint possession behind all this; why should I believe *you*? Did your grandmother leave a will? You know, the document people draft to allocate their possessions after their death and…"

"Yes," I interrupted once again. "I will bring it on the day of our appointment. I just wanted to gather some information before…"

"Good. In this case, let me get the appointment book. On that day, I will need to see a real document testifying to your quality as heir: I am thinking, most notably, and above all, about the will, about some proof of your identity, as well as of your relation with the *decujus*, and also—wait, I might as well give you the standard document list…"

He stood up, turned his back to me to grab a file above his head. I told myself that I only had a few seconds to act.

I pushed back the Louis-something chair, pulled the hammer out of my pocket and with a quick movement, hit him on the nape of his neck…

I felt like I had broken a dinosaur egg. Fernandes Quiroga jerked about, first falling on his desk and ending up on the floor, completely knocked out, with blood squirting on his white shirt.

In spite of my sudden fear, I started ransacking the room.

The drawers were littered with papers, but there were no bank notes. I even discovered a gun, which caused me more anguish. Fernandes Quiroga could have shot me, I told myself. It was the first time I saw a firearm up close.

I broke a large vase and a wooden box, no luck. I took several frames off the wall because, in the movies and in *Blek le Roc* comic strips, wealthy people always hid their safes behind paintings. Yet I found no safe like in the movies or *Blek le Roc* comic strips.

Then I opened a door that led to another, smaller room. I switched on the light and noticed a sofa-bed in a corner. I imagined Master Quiroga made love to his mistress from He-Who-Drinks-Water-Is-An-Idiot on it. There were a fridge and a hot plate there too. After that I happened upon a pile of folders, all well sealed; trembling, I toppled them. Finally I gave up and left the office at high speed, without glancing at the notary, who was hiccupping and regurgitating blood. I took my hammer, which had ended up near the front door, and ran down the stairs four steps at a time, still in the dark.

The caretaker was no longer in his room. Just then, a taxi parked in front of the building. The notary's young mistress stepped out of it. She might very well have caught me, had I not fallen flat on my face on the garden grass. She paid her fare and headed toward the building's main door.

That day, I walked from the fancy neighborhood back to my dwelling, a hut made out of planks I had built without proper authorization at the time, not far from the stream that cuts our city in two.

Master Fernandes Quiroga survived this assault. I no longer saw him in the streets of He-Who-Drinks-Water-Is-An-Idiot. Mindful of his reputation like all those from the center of town, he did not file a complaint. A few radio stations and newspapers in our country and the country over there mentioned my act, but at the time it was attributed to my idol and Great Master, Angoualima…

4.

It's always struck me that my large hands were made to kill, to wind individuals whose mugs I didn't like, those whose social position I envied and especially those who, in my book, were sullying the peace and quiet of my native corner with their dealings. I am convinced that Angoualima also carried this ideal deep inside him: to restore honor to He-Who-Drinks-Water-Is-An-Idiot…

I have my doubts about theories claiming to explain the behavior of people like me as the result of a disturbed past, a corrupted youth. Could it really be that my willpower has no part in what I undertake? That my entire life has been drawn in advance so that I am only following a path established by a force above me? Let me just laugh for a moment! People talk and have no clue how far they are from reality! Am I going to listen to them—*me*? Am I going to give credit to these ratiocinations?

They claim to be analyzing crimes, but have they committed even one? What kind of nonsense is that?

Me, I'm not under the influence of these theories, which I've heard several times in our city's criminal hearings—

hearings during which I became certain that public prosecutors were only after their own success. I know what I'm talking about. Inside my rectangular head is grey matter, not straw to burn.

As soon as I turned eighteen, then, I attended trials that featured blood and loss of life. I felt I was going to the movies because we had to stand in line, except that at the courthouse the shows were free and the actors stood a few feet away from us, just like at the theater. This passion had not occurred to me by chance. I wanted to familiarize myself with the faces of the criminals in our urban area. I wanted to know what was special about them, whether I could be like them, and whether I could recognize myself in the acts they had perpetrated. I considered them my brothers or sisters and shed tears—not at the evocation of their childhoods, but mostly because I was convinced that I was the one at the defendant's table.

I strolled around the courthouse, closely reading the dates of upcoming hearings, admiring lawyers' robes and decrying those worn by prosecutors because I told myself they were always the ones who decided everything—not judges or juries, whom you didn't even hear. Except, that is, for the president of the court. In my opinion, he rang his hand-bell much too long, asking for silence after the criminal and his escort of stone-faced policemen entered the room and created a stir.

Our city's big courthouse had thus become the site of my wanderings, my laboratory of human feelings. I lost myself in sinister, barely lit corridors. I strained to hear a family quarrel, a widow or an orphan cry. In general I noticed that anxiety could be read on the faces of people who were appearing in court even if they were certain to prevail. The victim's family always felt that the culprit had not been heavily condemned, while the perpetrator's clan cried foul, promising to take the case as far as it would go by getting "a relative who works in the President of the Republic's office" to intervene.

Just as a good Christian was supposed to go to church, I was convinced that this courthouse was my place of worship, the only place where I would cross paths with beings from my world, who were hounded by Destiny and trapped by the judgment of men, but ready to break free of their chains to better "shit on society," as the Great Master said in his time…

Several cases come to mind. That of Ted Louko, the man who had murdered his spouse with the help of an electrical screwdriver after a fit of jealousy, is the one that impressed me most. This man inspired pity in me because he was a poor workman. I had just then finished my apprenticeship in the sheet-iron and auto-body trade, and thought I might one day be the workman he was. A year had passed since my assault on the notary–real estate agent Fernandes Quiroga, and it had been forgotten quickly, due to the increasingly regular and sadistic crimes committed by the Great Master Angoualima.

Because Ted Louko suspected his wife to be the lover of one of his apprentices, he lost his head and did the deed at five in the morning while his spouse was asleep, a victim of the sleeping pill the cuckolded workman had slipped in her beer.

With an eloquence that mesmerized the audience, the public prosecutor, one of the most feared in our city, led the jury to believe that Ted Louko had been programmed to kill since his childhood and that he was a perpetual menace to society. The last words of this defender of the law's address echoed in the chamber for a long time. These remarks, and the timbre of his voice, hoarse and self-assured, have remained with me:

Yes, ladies and gentlemen of the court, in a moment you will hear arguments for the defense. But can they lull us into sleep and, with a magic wand, erase the horror and aggravation felt by all of this country's citizens? Does eloquence render a crime null and void? Here lies the question, ladies and gentlemen of the court! What are words worth in the face of the cruelty of facts? As far as I am concerned, I do not trust lawyers' flamboyant gestures. What we have here, let me remind you, is a sordid crime committed by the individual who is in front of you. Let no one try to tickle our ears with lyrical poetry...

What more is there to say, ladies and gentlemen of the court? This man is a stain on society, and as I demonstrated by going back into his muddy past, this man is fundamentally asocial. He resents each and every one of us for our normal childhoods. All the same, although he knows how to distinguish what is humane from what is barbarian, he has nonetheless, and with full knowledge of the facts, chosen his side—that of the paleolithic age. As someone once wrote, as far as he's concerned, "Man does not descend from the ape, he is turning into one!"

Yes, ladies and gentlemen of the court, you all know that if I vowed to serve this country's justice, it was in part to rid our society of all its riff-raff, of which the man who is being prosecuted today is the most fully realized incarnation.

At the end of the day, ladies and gentlemen of the

court, given that our country does not, alas, have any punishment beyond the death penalty, I can only request this sentence, and am doing it with a feeling of great frustration. I thank you…

In the chamber, some people who were not used to the rituals of the courthouse ventured to clap, to the great joy of the public prosecutor, who was positively suffocating with false modesty. The president of the court's little hand-bell put an end to their enthusiasm. The judge threatened to have the chamber evacuated, reminding us that this wasn't Anselmi Stadium and that we should reserve our applause for the next game between our national team and that of the country over there…

Well, a few years after this trial, I would like to tell this public prosecutor that, by nature, I too detest society. I don't give a damn about my past, which he would deem *muddy*. I cannot stand to see people teeming in the neighborhood of my youth. I am attached to this land that I take as mother and father, for wont of having had real parents. I am responsible for its honor, its reputation. Whoever speaks ill of He-Who-Drinks-Water-Is-An-Idiot offends me personally. Yes, I would have liked to live alone in this city and stroll at every hour of the day or night without encountering another soul. That's why, until the day I accepted that Germaine was coming to live with me, I always lived alone. I wallowed in my solitude and derived from it a kind of satisfaction I wouldn't have traded for anything in the world. Everything that happened outside meant little to me. My workshop was what counted most for me. It was society that didn't understand me. As a result, aware that I was in the right, I had to erect a fortress between society and myself…

I have not lost my lone-wolf habits. I still barricade my plot's main bamboo door and look three or four times down the street. I do not allow any client to enter my place of business with his wrecked car. I take care of this myself. Once it is fixed, I deliver it to his residence. That way, my ivory tower is preserved from indiscreet looks. I know that my neighbors, who by the way I am not eager to know, must curse me when I bang on scrap iron, sometimes late into the night...

5.

To kill—a verb I have worshiped since coming of age. Fundamentally, all the small jobs I carried out were done in the hope of later being able to conjugate this verb in its most immediate and fully realized form.

Of course, as of today, I cannot take credit for any murder. To my great surprise, after the failed act against Master Fernandes Quiroga, there was even a lull when the idea of doing harm no longer appealed to me. I was plunged in torpor by a sort of Christian goodness. I was like a lost mollusk. Was this a start toward tolerance?

I cannot find an explanation for this period of dead quiet, these days when I was ashamed to exist, to bear the name Grégoire Nakobomayo, a name I owe, no doubt, to a lottery in the institutions where picked-up children are parked.

I knew I wasn't myself. I knew that I was no more than an empty shell, an ordinary being, cultivating his garden on the margin of society.

I would look at my hands with dismay and reproach myself for certain earlier deeds, such as stealing old people's wallets or IDs, piercing my adoptive brother's eye because he wanted to abuse me and many others still. These ones were of lesser importance, but as a matter of fact they strengthened my experience so that I could one day arrive at a more coherent gesture, with a result that would suit me and, by the same token, delight Angoualima, my idol, in his grave.

In these moments of depression, I would sob in my shop and, raging, bang the mallet against beat-up cars. To calm down, I would go out at night and hang around He-Who-Drinks-Water-Is-An-Idiot's alleys. I would approach a whore and relieve myself like one who hasn't touched a woman in centuries. Having liberated myself, I would be gripped by remorse for wasting my seed. I scrutinized the streetwalker with hate and held back the urge to crush her carotids with hands that had finally grown bigger but lacked a credible criminal reference.

During the first hours of the next day, I would head toward the cemetery of The-Dead-Who-Are-Not-Allowed-To-Sleep. I would spend an eternity in front of the Great Master's grave and tell him about my days and nights…

I didn't understand why I couldn't claim at least one successful murder in my favor. Every one of my projects ended in a fiasco or was attributed to some lame scoundrel from He-Who-Drinks-Water-Is-An-Idiot. During that time, I took all the blame that Angoualima's ghost directed at me without flinching, because his ghost is more demanding and more ruthless than he himself was when he was alive.

One day, exasperated by this lethargic state, I looked at myself in the shower after masturbating without feeling any real pleasure. I saw the face of an incompetent, of a clumsy individual, and hit my fist hard against the mirror. It fell to pieces. Blood dripped from my severed veins and I started licking it until the last drop, promising myself to achieve my goal, sooner or later…

Now I get up every day and whisper Angoualima. I go to bed every night and whisper Angoualima. He hears me, I know. He has become the father I have not known and haven't tried to know, for fear of forever losing my identity.

I have returned to the Great Master's grave on several occasions lately to collect my thoughts. I have told him about everything that's weighing on my heart, but have refrained from announcing the crime I am planning against Germaine on December 29. Otherwise—I know him well—he would have to express his opinion again and perhaps yell at me because I am taking too much time to proceed.

I know that, from the bottom of his grave, Angoualima the Great Master sees everything. But never mind. This time I am taking the risk of concealing my project from him. The crime I am about to commit belongs to me first and foremost because I want to save my neighborhood from dishonor. I wouldn't want the Great Master to imagine that he had anything to do with it. I want to conceive of everything from beginning to end and plant my foot upon my victim as a sign of satisfaction, like a hunter happy to have killed his first big game. My crime will be more beautiful than those of my idol…

6.

Angoualima had experience, I'll admit that. He had been lucky to learn the ropes of the trade in the country over there, where he had spent his youth. Born like me in He-Who-Drinks-Water-Is-An-Idiot, the "picked-up child" that he was, would become in turn a pedicab driver, a kitchen hand and a fishmonger on the bank of the Mayi River before anyone heard of him around here. He was then renowned for his trick of misleading those who were looking for him by having shoes made for himself that left footprints going in the wrong direction. No bandit had thought of this before he did, and this only served to strengthen his legend.

We were far from imagining that he would leave the country over there and cross back over the Mayi River to come live in his native country and distinguish himself as one of the most ingenious murderers we had ever known.

Back in He-Who-Drinks-Water-Is-An-Idiot, Angoualima started with spectacular robberies in the residences of the white aid cadres from the center of town. He mastered mpini, the ability to make himself invisible by reciting formulas that even our country's charlatans and witch doctors found unfathomable. He had in his possession a dry herb that he would burn. It would put the owners of the houses that he "visited" in the middle of the night to sleep. He would then take his time, sit down, turn on the TV, turn up the music as loud as possible, open the fridge, heat up some food and eat while his victims snored like mopeds with damaged mufflers. Next he would shove the husband to one corner of the bed, flip the wife over, and drive his thing into her. Journalists had unanimously nicknamed his thing "the fifth limb" because it was as big as Mayi River fishermen's biceps. He always left twenty-five Cuban cigars burning in the raped woman's thing. Before leaving, his truck full of goods, he would sign Angoualima on the residence's walls...

I was coming of age and beginning to visit our city's courthouses, and I have to tell you, we were living through the period of the greatest terror, during which Angoualima sent statuettes with severed heads to his future victims. Not one month would go by without someone discovering two or three heads of men or women on the wild coast, Cuban cigars in their mouths, their hair combed, the rest of their bodies a few feet away. Angoualima saw to it that these faces appeared to be smiling and their eyes open, enjoying the cigar screwed between their lips.

In spite of the canvassing the police undertook in the area of the wild coast, they did not succeed in arresting my idol, who took perverse pleasure in playing hide-and-seek with these poor uniformed men. As soon as they had their backs turned, they were called again a half hour later to come verify the presence of the heads of men and women lined up on the fine sandy beach. And they noticed the special footprints of Angoualima's famous shoes. The policemen followed them excitedly, like hunting dogs, and they didn't understand that they directed them toward the water, as if the country's enemy number one, who was described as a monster, came out of the sea with a giant fish tail...

At that time, of course, he was the only topic that both the national press and the press of the country over there would cover. My idol was more famous than our President of the Republic and our musicians combined. And this even though it was the one-party year, when the portrait of our head of state could be seen at every intersection in our country. This was also the year when, coming from the country over there, we discovered great musicians on the order of Rochereau Tabu Ley, who appeared at the mythic Olympia theater in Paris; Luambo Makiadi, a.k.a. Franco, and his unequaled fifths on the guitar; Lita Bembo with his Salamander shoes; and Sam Mangwana and his afro. Finally, it was the era of such musical groups as Lipua-Lipua, Stukas with Lita Bembo, Zaïko Langa Langa with Manuaku Waku, etc. Angoualima stole the headlines from them in our country and the country over there. There was no more room for other news items, and journalists even had to shorten the sacrosanct political pages dedicated to the president in order to have more space to recount in detail the Great Master's lightning ascent.

Life is not what it used to be. We were waiting with bated breath for Angoualima's next stunning deed...

The population was curious to see my see my idol's face at long last. This is why the tabloids sold like hot cakes when they announced they were publishing pictures of him in their center spreads.

Can I just say: Could these even be called pictures? Where on earth did these people take them? Was the Great Master such an idiot that he would accept being the target of flashbulbs?

Sure, there were pictures. I don't deny it. People believe

everything that's published in the newspaper. They may have their doubts about radio and television, but not about the information and images published in a newspaper. It's written, therefore it's serious, therefore it's been verified, and after all, these people who know how to write are not imbeciles, etc.

In fact these were vague and debatable images, montages that sent readers to seek the help of big magnifying glasses to better make out every detail. Even a pregnant woman's first ultrasound was clearer...

As a result, every man in the street could have been Angoualima. What am I saying, every man? Maybe not just every man, because people also said that he was able to change sex depending on the crime he was about to commit. Better yet, that he was able to transform himself into a teenager, and that every time this kid was asked to run an errand into an estate, he turned back into Angoualima in order to act.

Capitalizing on the general confusion, the pathetic villains of He-Who-Drinks-Water-Is-An-Idiot passed themselves off as my idol. Irritated, the Great Master had to clean house on both of our city's banks. Every day, we would discover the head of a murderer who, the previous day, had claimed he was the real Angoualima. With all this going on, our city's scoundrels were feeling more threatened than the ordinary citizens did. Parents forbade their children to utter this cursed name, which returned to people's lips and fed conversations in markets, bars and funeral homes. Some even claimed that Angoualima had simply been invented by some citizens who did not want to pay taxes, without anyone understanding the link between taxes and the heads of victims that were being picked up along the wild coast...

Very quickly Angoualima became synonymous with murder, invisibility, theft, rape and with the ability to leave the police behind. Popular songs banned by the government perpetuated this myth of the faceless murderer. No one knew in which of the city's districts the Great Master resided. People talked about He-Who-Drinks-Water-Is-An-Idiot or Sotexco, then about the Plateau, or again about Talangaï, Poto-Poto, Ouenzé or Moungali…

In short, he lived everywhere. And people also imagined he lived underground because the worm was his totem; that he lived at the bottom of the sea because the shark was his totem; that he lived in treetops because the bird was his totem; that he lived in freight trains because, in order to fool the police, he was able to turn himself into a package or blend into a herd of sheep; that he lived in cemeteries because that was where he drew his supernatural strength; that he lived in the hollows of baobab trees because the rodent was his totem.

People would report that he was an herbivore; hmm, no, that he had to be a cannibal; hmm, no, that he didn't eat; hmm, no, that he could refrain from eating for months or be content with just one peanut and one glass of water every other day! They added that he came out only during nights when the moon was full. And during tornadoes, he took on the appearance of a shivering white puppy that inspired such pity that any Good Samaritan would take it into his residence to keep it warm…

At this time when television was still in black and white, during a program that even now counts amongst the small screen's most intense moments in our country, one man, his face uncovered, claimed he had crossed paths with the Great

Master Angoualima at one o'clock in the morning near the stream that cuts our city in two. And he declared that Angoualima was not an ordinary being, which everybody knew already. If it was to say this that the man had been invited, the entire city would have taken the set by storm to repeat over and over again that my idol was not an ordinary man!

What was surprising, however, was that the man in question swore on his deceased mother and father's heads that he had seen my idol with his own eyes, and that it wasn't a dream.

The interview, which he granted exclusively to the journalist, remains engraved in our memories. It is reportedly dissected every year in our journalism schools, where its technique is called "Well then? Trust me!"…

"Well then," the journalist began, his strong accent typical of the north of the country. "You have seen him with your very own eyes. What kind of a face does he have?"

"He has two faces," answered the interviewee. "Yes, I saw two faces just as if I were seeing you here twice over, trust me!"

"Well then, what do you mean, two faces? Explain this to us, we find it hard to understand! Answer while looking into camera A, please…"

"Yes, two faces! One in front and one in back, Angoualima can look both in front of him and behind him, trust me!"

"Well then, two faces, therefore four eyes, therefore four ears, therefore…"

"Yes, therefore everything you say… Yes, that's it exactly. And what's more, his four eyes, four ears, two mouths, two noses are well well-regulated, trust me!"

"Well then, of these two faces, which one is in the front

and which one is in the back? Answer while looking into camera B, please…"

"It depends on his mood, trust me!"

"Well then, how does he manage to speak with two mouths?"

"One mouth begins the sentence and the other one finishes it, trust me!"

"Magnificent! Magnificent! Hmm. Please forgive me, dear viewers. Well then, how does he manage to eat with two mouths?"

"I told you that everything about him was well-regulated! One mouth chews, transfers the food into the other, which swallows it, trust me!"

"Very impressive! Really very impressive! Well then, what happens if he becomes sick?"

"Please, sir, what are you saying here? Do you understand what you're talking about? Angoualima cannot become sick entirely, given that when one part of his body suffers, the other is always in good health, trust me!"

"Quite astounding! Really quite astounding! Well then, how does he go about making love, given that you seem to be hinting to our viewers and myself that he has two *things* instead of one like normal men? Answer while looking mostly into camera C, please…"

"He always makes love to two women, who get down on all fours and present their behinds to him. As for him, he gets down on his knees in the middle and performs violent back-and-forth movements. Thus he satisfies both women at the same time, trust me!"

"Well, what a man he is! Hmm. Forgive me, dear viewers, it's emotion speaking… Well then, more concretely, because this is a question viewers must be asking themselves, and that I myself am asking myself, and therefore you must answer while still looking into camera C: how does he go about shitting? Because he surely has to shit like we do, doesn't he?"

"Come on, it's simple: one anus for shitting on even days and the other anus for shitting on odd days, trust me!"

"Hell! Well then, another concrete question that viewers must be asking themselves and that I myself am asking myself: how does he go about peeing? Because he must surely pee like we do! Answer while still looking into camera C, please…"

"He pees every hour: one *thing* for peeing even hours and another *thing* for peeing odd hours, trust me!"

"Quite unbelievable! Really, quite unbelievable! Well then, a dumb but practical question that springs to my mind, and doubtlessly to viewers' minds: how then does he manage with his pants, given that pants, as you know, are made for those who have only one *thing*, when you seem to be hinting to viewers and to myself that he has two *things*, one in front and one in back or vice versa? Answer while still looking into camera C, please…"

"I saw him wearing pants with two zippers: one in front, one in back, and vice versa, as you say, trust me!"

"What imagination! Really, what imagination! Well then, still among the practical questions I am asking myself and feel our viewers are asking themselves too. While answering you can choose between camera A or camera B but absolutely not camera C, please. How then does he manage to sleep and not suffocate himself given that he has one face in front and one face in back or vice versa? Because he has to sleep like we do, you do agree, don't you?"

"For sleeping, he has two options he uses during the same night: he sleeps standing up during even hours and on the side during odd hours, trust me!"

"Unheard of! Really, unheard of! Well then, in the same type of question: when he sleeps, how does it work out, do the two faces sleep at the same time? Camera A or B but absolutely not C, I beg you!"

"His faces take turns sleeping: one sleeps during one hour while the other face stands guard during that hour, and so on until dawn, trust me!"

"Quite genius! Really, quite genius! Hmm. Excuse my emotion, dear viewers… Well then, the moment that we are all waiting for has come. Answer while looking into camera A for five seconds, camera B for five seconds and camera C for five seconds, because you must look all of this country's television viewers straight in the eyes: can we know your name, given that you're becoming famous from one day to the next, being the only person to have seen Angoualima?"

"I will not tell you my name, trust me!"

"Well then, why?"

"That's the way it is, trust me!"

"Well then, tell us: is it because you're frightened of Angoualima, frightened for your family, for those close to you, or is it out of simple modesty, which viewers would understand easily?"

"No, I fear only one thing: that the sky will fall on my head, trust me!"

"Well then, if Angoualima were listening to you at this very moment, when it is 11:58 GMT by my watch and viewers' watches, what would you say to him?"

"It is 11:58 GMT by my watch too, and I would say to Angoualima that he is a monster, a rogue, a coward, a peasant, a ghost without a cemetery and that he will die a tragic death, trust me!"

"Well then, is Angoualima really a monster? Aren't you pushing it a bit?"

"Yes, he's a repugnant monster, I am saying it again! The guy has no pity, trust me!"

"Well then, really repugnant?"

"Yes, that's what I'm saying, trust me!"

"Well then, are you responsible for what you are saying at this very moment when it has just turned 11:59 GMT by my watch and our viewers' watches?"

"Yes, I am responsible for what I am saying and it's also 11:59 GMT by my watch, trust me!"

"Well then, aren't you afraid of Angoualima's anger? You do know, don't you, that this man listens to everything that's being said with regards to his name in this city, hmmm?"

"No, I'm not afraid of him at all, because I have told you that the only thing I fear is that the sky will fall on my head one day, trust me!"

"Well then, you really are a good guy, a courageous guy, a hero. We can put it this way, don't you think?"

"Yes, you can put it this way, trust me!"

"Well then, the interview is over, then, but don't leave the three cameras yet because there may be viewers in the back country who have just come home and therefore have not seen the beginning of this exclusive interview."

"I thank you for inviting me, trust me!"

"Well then, we thank you for your bravery, for your courage, and for your patriotic heroism. Stay with us to comment on the day's news after a short commercial break…"

The day after this memorable interview, this man and the journalist's heads were found on the wild coast, each of them with a Cuban cigar screwed between the lips. From then on this part of the coast would be called "Well then? Trust me!"…

7.

When my idol began to eradicate the villains in this city who were usurping his reputation, the police were caught short and lingered instead of rushing to catch the man who was then nicknamed the "Judge of Darkness."

It's true that he killed innocent folks, some said, but he made the work of our police force easier all the same. Wasn't the government itself divided on that point? Didn't the police prefect congratulate himself on the declining crime rate? What this representative of the local authorities ignored was that Angoualima had now decided to bring the rate of crimes and misdemeanors in our urban area up or down all by himself.

When he was invited on television to deplore the murders of the "Well then?" journalist and his heroic and patriotic "Trust me!" guest, our police prefect commended the effectiveness of his men working in the field to push back crime. High on his own euphoria, he announced new measures, the most original of which he said concerned my idol and Great Master Angoualima: a special team, trained in Israel, had been put together to capture him dead or alive. The population was called upon to participate, with a huge reward for the person who could help authorities arrest the Great Master or, at the very least, find out where he slept.

The office the police prefect opened and called Immediate Capture of Angoualima (ICA) had to close down after a week. Indeed, our city's residents no longer wanted to play the national lottery—they preferred lining up in front of the ICA spinning nutty stories they said they'd heard from someone who had seen someone who had seen someone who had seen Angoualima!

What in fact made the prefect decide to close down the

ICA, we were to learn later on, was that Angoualima himself also lined up there several days in a row. And when, inside the office, he asserted that he was Angoualima, that they first had to give him his reward of several million CFA francs before capturing or killing him, the detectives convulsed with laughter each and every time, taking him for a bum from the banks of our stream. For all my Great Master's explanations that he was Angoualima, no one wanted to believe him. He was then thrown outside, sometimes with a kick in the rear…

Angoualima sent all our city precincts and the police prefect a humiliating letter, in which he said that there was to be absolutely no thanking him for all the work he was doing in the policemen's stead, and that the policeman who would catch him wasn't born yet, given that each time he had shown up in person at the ICA, the detectives had been incapable of arresting him. In the same letter, he said he was also curious to know how the ICA was going to capture or kill him when it lacked any description of his face or, conversely, when it had as many as there were people in our city, which is to say more than five hundred thousand souls, not counting people from the country over there who have settled in our midst! As a post script to the letter, he announced an action that would cover our police in unprecedented shame.

A few days later, in spite of the prefect's instructions to hush up the matter, there were leaks about a theft of ammunitions and firearms from several precincts. How could the envelope be pushed this far? My idol had signed his name on the precincts' facades.

Given the recklessness of this action, the whole country now believed that Angoualima was in fact none other than a rotten cop at the helm of a criminal organization. Our city now teemed with weapons, and the population barricaded itself at nightfall. The special team our police prefect boasted about turned the city inside out without picking up my idol and Great Master's trail, and there was still no description of him.

In the days that followed this historic theft in the precincts, policemen were booed as they went about walking their beats. They were reminded that they had better focus their efforts on finding Angoualima rather than strutting around the neighborhoods, armed to the teeth, hounding pathetic hemp dealers and second-hand dealers. Here and there people shouted, "Long live Angoualima!"

Still there were no massacres, contrary to what the authorities feared. They had taken up the matter quickly, transforming it into a major election issue.

My idol didn't use the weapons that were in his possession. It took another couple of weeks before Angoualima sent letters to the precincts in question so they could reclaim their weapons and ammunitions on the wild coast, in the spot where one found heads without bodies, with Cuban cigars screwed between the lips.

Oh I mean, talk about ridicule! The country watched on television as, tails between their legs, the policemen picked up the stolen weapons and ammunitions and packed them away in military trucks.

Angoualima was still on the run.

I counted a few jobs to my credit already. If I remember correctly, this was the time when my assault with a hammer on the notary–real estate agent Fernandes Quiroga was credited to Angoualima. I lived through this with frustration. And how!

I rejoiced that people thought this act of enough importance that they would attribute it to my idol and Great Master. At least the city had become aware of it. Angoualima did not deny this offense. Even when a journalist dared conclude that the assault on Master Fernandes Quiroga was so low that it didn't look like his doing, Angoualima let these analyses pass. This surprised me very much because, knowing him, he should have beheaded the first person to suggest his responsibility in this minor aggression. After that he should have gone after the analyst who got tangled up in risky comparisons, as if he really knew the way my idol and Great Master operated. His silence alarmed me more and more. There was no punishment for all this, no answer to it. Angoualima was no longer refuting the small acts of banditry people pinned on him even though he hadn't perpetrated them.

Thus, our city's villains operated with complete immunity, aware that their heinous crimes would only be added on to my idol's already much-revised tab.

A vehicle was stolen? It was Angoualima! A bad driver ran over a pedestrian and fled? It was Angoualima! A body was found in the stream that cuts our city in two? It was Angoualima!

One day, I think it was a Sunday night, but no matter, I was following Listeners Speak Out, a very popular radio show that even people in the country over there listened to. The guest of the day, who was visiting the city, was a professor of criminology at the only university in our country, Me-I-

Know-Everything-Because-You-Don't-Understand-Anything High University, which is located in the political capital, more than five hundred kilometers from my hometown. The show's theme was enticing:

Angoualima: Myth or Reality? React!

And this professor got on my nerves because he brought everything back to himself, his own person, his intelligence, in front of journalists who were astounded by his knowledge.

"Gentlemen," he said. "I will tell you that in my position as a devoted follower of the Italian school of criminology, I have been fascinated by a book that I recommend to everybody, *L'Uomo Delinquente (The Criminal Man)*, by Cesare Lombroso, and by its magnificent theory about the born criminal. Angoualima has his place in the pages of this mythical book, a foundational text for the manner in which we perceive the criminal being. The actions of Angoualima, this sadly famous son of a bitch, bring to mind a number of European cases I discovered while attending the Poitiers law school... I am thinking especially of a young criminal called Baptiste Laborie, who once brought his brother's head to Saint-Louis Hospital to have a doctor embalm it! I am also thinking of Sadilleck with his butcher's knife—because he truly was a butcher—who went after an unfortunate traveler on the Paris-Boulogne Express! I am not forgetting Henry Lestevens, the woman-killer who haunted Paris's ring roads in search of his future victims, generally naïve working women to whom he promised marriage before killing them... .

"But we had better come back to Angoualima. I think your viewers are eagerly awaiting my views about this scoundrel... I am going to sketch out a detailed analysis of this madman's behavior *hic et nunc*... If you will allow me, I will do so in two main parts, which themselves will be divided into subparts, which might call for diametrically opposed but not necessarily antithetical subdivisions and conclusions…"

My God! And the Great Master's name was being taken in vain. Angoualima's actions were being compared to those of bandits, of famous European criminals whose names I was hearing for the first time. The journalists held back their laughter. Intervening in the most complete cacophony, listeners generally supported their arguments. I felt these attacks deep inside of me. I could not let my idol take these low blows.

Furious, I ran outside my home until I reached the first phone booth. I manhandled an old man with a cane. He was calling his grandson to ask him to send a money order so that he could finish his roof, which had been blown off by the tornado.

I had trouble getting through: the station's switchboard was saturated with calls from all around our country and the country over there.

After half an hour I finally succeeded and was on the line with the studio.

"Yes, sir," said one of the journalists. "Please introduce yourself. Where are you calling from, then? Are you in the back country perhaps? The line is really very bad. Do you want to ask the professor a question?"

"I am Angoualima and you can go fuck yourself," I said in a voice I had rendered sepulchral by wrapping part of my shirt around the receiver.

There was a moment of silence, during which I heard moving chairs and whispered conversation.

"Hello?" I raged. "Have you lost your nerve or what?"

The whispered conversation went on with the buzzing of

microphones. The star journalist cleared his throat and got ahold of himself.

"Listen, sir, let's be serious: you are not Angoualima! And besides, what would prove to us that you are? If you're not bringing anything constructive to this respectable program, which is honored by the presence of a great professor who has studied and become a laureate in Europe, we are going to take another call. There are people waiting: the switchboard is red!"

"Ah really? Okay, I am taking note of the fact that there are cretins out there who do not know what they're talking about and whose memory is short," I said, with menace in my voice. "Do you then want me to prove that I am Angoualima as early as tonight, when you leave the station, mister journalist of my ass?"

"You're just an impostor, a cowardly individual who hides behind a cloak of anonymity so that…"

"Okay, at least those who are close to you will already know where to look for your warthog head with a Cuban cigar between the lips!"

"Listen, sir, you are so vulgar that we might feel obliged to hang up on you and tell you to stuff your cigars you know where, and…"

"Very good! Very good! I am going to hang up, then, and take listeners as my witnesses. From this moment on, you are a dead man, a corpse without a head, I am telling you! Good show, gentlemen!"

"Mister, mister Angoualima, wait! Angoualima… er… can you hear us? Mister Angoualima, you understand that this program is a news show, and as a matter of principle we are only reporting the news insofar as…"

"You have insulted me, you shithead! You have put my reputation in doubt, and that's a crime, mister criminology laureate and mister journalist of my ass!"

"I mean, er... Hello? Hello? Hello? Don't hang up, please, mister Angoualima! Are you still on the line? Hello? Hello?..."

"You have thirty seconds by my watch! I am waiting for your public apology, mister journalist, otherwise begin your prayers as soon as the show is over, because today's prayer is your last, I'm telling you... !"

"But I... in fact I..."

"Well, fuck! Are you going to apologize or not?"

"Yes, mister Angoualima, so... I want, I think, er, that..."

"There's nine seconds left and my twelve fingers are not made for tickling the phone!"

"In the name of the radio station president, of all my colleagues, of the editor-in-chief, of the program director, of the musical programming director, of the special correspondents, of the technical personnel, of our advertisers, of our sponsors, of the secretary, of the interns, of the freelancers, of the cleaning lady, of the caretaker and of the professor, if we have made remarks that offended you, we would like to express our most sincere apologies and..."

"This is too long, sir! Be brief, I'm in a hurry, there are people waiting to offer me their heads!"

"But, what do you want me to say, mister Angoualima? Still I was very..."

"Say: Forgive us, mister Angoualima, you are the Great Master of crime and the guardian of He-Who-Drinks-Water-Is-An-Idiot's honor!"

"But, mister Angoualima, do you realize that..."

"That's it for you! What kind of cigar do you prefer for your shithead, a *Cohiba* or a *Romeo y Julieta*?"

"Wait! Wait! *Forgive us, mister Angoualima, you are the Great Master of crime and the guardian of He-Who-Drinks-Water-Is-An-Idiot's honor!*"

"Thank you, sir, that's very kind of you! You are forgiven, but just for now."

"We said what you wanted to hear, mister Angoualima!"

"What? What do I hear? You're now raising your voice against the Great Master Angoualima? Is that how I should take this, shithead?"

"No, mister Angoualima."

"You say: No, Great Master!"

"No, Great Master, I would not dare to…"

"Very good, we understand each other!"

"We in this studio are rejoicing, Great Master…"

"That's good! It's amazing how cooperative journalists can be when they want to!"

"You know, Great Master, the truth is, and our listeners know this well, that we are only doing our duty. What's more, far from denigrating you, this program rather gives you a historic dimension that other criminals would envy…"

"Silence! These kinds of speeches are not for me!"

"Understood, Great Master…"

"Good. Now do you know what you still need to do so that your insults are washed away once and for all?"

"No, Great Master, we thought we had already done our best and…"

"I ask that your shit theme music come on: this show is over!"

"Sorry, mister Great Master, er, mister Angoualima, we haven't followed very well. You are saying that…"

"You've heard correctly: it's over, this show! I no longer want to hear this old fart of a professor whose breath stinks when he opens his mouth to pronounce my name. What is this? Who do you think I am? So now his Italian school is going to explain what I, *me,* am doing?"

"No, mister Angoualima. What's more, these were

examples the professor drew from white criminals, whereas you, mister Angoualima, you are not white and…"

"The show is over! You may have saved your shit journalist's head, but as far as your testicles and your *thing* are concerned, it's not all in the bag yet, you see what I mean, journalist of my ass? I hope you've had children already. I'm hanging up!"

There was an icy silence on the air.

Outside I saw people running as one herd from their plots of land, hanging on to their transistor radios. In a matter of seconds, my intervention had gone all around the city, the country and the country over there, and I was convinced that Angoualima was listening to me.

When the end theme music of *Listeners Speak Out* came on, I could not hold back a victorious cry. I wondered where this temerity and self-assured speaking manner had come from. I was more than inspired that night.

All the national press and even that of the country over there spoke about my phone call, but it was the real Angoualima who benefited from it.

To this day, whenever this episode is evoked in the press or mentioned as part of our national radio's collection of howlers, my phone prowess is credited to the real Angoualima. And given that no one in the country has ever heard my idol's voice, people believe that his timbre is the one I achieved that Sunday by wrapping the telephone receiver in part of my shirt…

Why didn't the Great Master react to all this with the quickness he is known for? He never gave any additional news of himself. I wasn't going to keep shadowing him all my life.

In truth, I was becoming increasingly convinced that a

page of our criminal history was being turned.

What followed would prove me right.

Angoualima was forgotten for at least two years, until the day when the national press and that of the country over there received an audio tape with these obscene words, "I shit on society," along with a letter in which my Great Master described where his body could be found after his suicide.

People first thought it a practical joke, a trap. Our television and that of the country over there, which had dispatched correspondents, thus tread very carefully toward the wharf, not far from the wild coast, and to their amazement discovered the body of a small man, lying down, arms crossed, eyes shut. He had six fingers on each hand and a harelip. His skull bulged in the back and his eyebrows were bushy. He had scars on his face and an old ram's goatee. The former members of the ICA recognized in him the dirty individual who had shown up several times in their office, back in the day.

Before dying, my idol had drawn a circle around himself, as if to explain that the loop had been looped, that the snake had bitten its tail…

Such is the image our country and the country over there have kept of my idol Angoualima, the man with twelve fingers.

His photographs are still being sold clandestinely. The police don't think twice about locking up those who buy them or take part in this distasteful trade. The members of the musical group the Brothers The-Same-People-Always-

Get-To-Eat-In-This-Shitty-Country all spent time in prison after their hit, which was produced in Europe but banned in our country and which young people could listen to thanks to Intercontinental Radio...

The Girl in White

1.

I still have in my possession the short news item from the newspaper *The Street Is Dying* relating my most recent deed against the girl in white, some three months ago. I would like to present my reasons for this failure, which annoys me to this day.

> *A nurse at Adolphe-Cissé Hospital was assaulted by a sex maniac upon her return home from work. A complaint was filed at the police station of the He-Who-Drinks-Water-Is-An-Idiot neighborhood.*

I am aware that the amateurism I demonstrated deserves blame. The day after the deed, I didn't let myself be overcome by despair, certain as I was that the radio was going to talk about it. Although Angoualima, very much in spite of himself, could have once again benefited from this action without having perpetrated it, he was dead, so it stood to reason that people would be talking about the advent of a new outlaw in our city. It was obvious, I had no doubt about it.

I told myself that there would finally be a report about the event, around midnight or one in the morning, to fill the empty hours during which listeners' ears are saturated with traditional music from the Pygmies of the former *Oubangui-Chari*.

Alas, it wasn't to be!

Disconcerted, I was about to fall asleep when a journalist, in a voice that was both nasal and throaty, started mumbling endless death announcements. People who for the most part had died "after a long illness." Parents who asked their relatives in the backcountry to hurry up and take the first train to be present for the burial...

In my workshop, I was, as usual, yelling "Oh, shit!" nonstop. This swear word calms me down, gives me the illusion that I am master of each situation, and allows me to reconnect with my vulgarity, which makes me feel most comfortable. You should always have a few magic words like oh, shit—otherwise, how could you get by, huh? What would it have cost them, these radio hosts and journalists, to talk about my crime that night? Did they want something more convincing? Had morals changed or something? I couldn't understand anything anymore.

I'm not the type who gets discouraged—oh no, definitely not. Another radio station was bound to talk about it, I told myself. I know that death announcements guarantee you'll have listeners but, come on, there are limits! Extolling in this manner people who've found nothing better to do than to croak "after a long illness," as if there were no other ways to die! It's a waste, and that's not all there is to life. This situation sickens me, personally. When I think that people like me sweat blood to do their jobs and take risks, and then no one gives us the least bit of play in the media! The victim always gets the lion's share, and that's unfair! I agree with whoever said you have to "let the dead bury the dead." We're told about such-and-such family regretfully announcing the death of so-and-so, and that a requiem mass will be held on February 24 in the chapel of He-Who-Drinks-Water-Is-An-Idiot, etc. It's all bluff. That's not the point. Oh, shit!

Me, I really wish that, one day, these announcements dwelled a little on the real reasons behind an individual's death instead of covering him with a shroud of modesty, even if he was just a poor redneck. On that day, we would see whether he really "died after a long illness."

Who are they kidding?

Therefore, being stubborn, I looked for other stations, but came upon what I had discovered previously: radio silence. I came out of my shop, where, beside myself, I was hitting the mallet hard against the damaged cars. I paced around the plot before finally coming into the house. I took a half-full bottle of beer out of the refrigerator and turned on the television. I sat down on the sofa bed. As if by chance, a long documentary about predatory animals was on. A lion was dismembering an antelope. A boa was working doggedly at swallowing a stag and was caught in his own trap as his prey's antlers made his task impossible. As a result, the documentary's narrator concluded, this big snake was going to die with his loot in his mouth, his appetite had been bigger than his stomach. Dryly, the narrator reminded viewers, "Before you climb up a tree, make sure you will be able to come down."

Was this documentary some sort of omen for me? I am not an animal. I am not a boa. Boas don't think, I am sure of that. They are driven by instinct. Me, I have always added reason to my actions. I can climb up a tree and come down with ease...

Okay. I have to put things in perspective as far as this failed job is concerned so that I don't compare it to the feats of the Great Master Angoualima. Don't imagine that I am a good-for-nothing, even if I can barely take credit for only a few infractions that, at worst, had I been arrested, would have gotten me into the district court of summary jurisdiction, where my hearing would have taken place after the hearings for rooster and papaya thieves.

So *The Street Is Dying* had dubbed me a "sex maniac"! What would the person who wrote this laconic and offensive text know about that? Personally, deep down, I wanted to kill this girl in white, and the rape was just a cherry on the cake, a little bit like when Angoualima was in the white aide cadres' residences. I was finally getting the opportunity to play in the big leagues and to no longer be content with the kid whose right eye I had pierced and the notary–real estate agent whose skull I had smashed all those years before. I had a golden opportunity to kill my first hooker. It was through *The Street Is Dying* that I learned the next day that she wasn't a hooker, but a nurse at Adolphe-Cissé Hospital.

Why indeed did I have designs on her? I had to start my project of cleaning up the He-Who-Drinks-Water-Is-An-Idiot district somewhere. My ambition would surely frighten those long in the trade, and Angoualima and his twelve fingers would turn in his grave. They would argue that such an initiative doesn't take place upon exiting a watering hole and that, in order to succeed, your balls need to be in the right place.

With hindsight, I tell myself that I had too much gin that night. That was negligent on my part. Drinking always makes you lose focus. This particular liquor arouses intense sexual desire in me. Consequently, the rape came first and the murder was relegated to second place.

As a matter of fact, stepping out of the bar called Take And Drink, This is The Cup of My Blood, I found myself at the very heart of the He-Who-Drinks-Water-Is-An-Idiot district, in the hope of finding a hot little mama and laying the first stone in my public health campaign. I walked along One-Hundred-Francs-Only Street, with its shanties made of wood planks and mountains of refuse just outside the lots. The night was dark, very dark, after a sultry day the likes of which we hadn't had for a long time in the city. I had given up on working in my shop and spent the day in various watering holes. Nevertheless, there came a time when you had to go back home and stop fattening up all these shopkeepers who congratulated themselves on a day when throats were dry throughout the city. My instinct told me this night wouldn't be like the others. My hands were swelling and I felt my veins were going to burst if I didn't do something, experience some great shock that would calm me down. I had to walk, breathe in some air. That's what I did.

At the corner of One-Hundred-Francs-Only and Daddy-Happiness-That's-Me Streets, in spite of the opaque darkness and thanks to her white clothing, I made out the silhouette of a woman, tall, straight, her purse tucked under her armpit. I said to myself: *"Hey, hey, she's a new one, this one—let's get closer and take a look!"* I noticed that her behind was really what I call, perhaps by professional idiosyncrasy, a *frame loaded with goodies*. It's clear that girls who don't have enough goodies on their frames don't hold any interest for me, and I wouldn't waste my time gratifying them with death. They can just wait to die after a long illness, as they say on the radio, and be part of the death announcements in the morning and at night. For me, when I want to have sex with a whore, it's the frame that's gotten things started. And when there's none, it's no use wasting your energy: you can be sure that, in bed, the girl will remain supine, as motionless as a wood plank, and will be counting the stars...

I know this street like the back of my hand and can even explain why, today, it's called One-Hundred-Francs-Only. It's because, in the old days, it was the girls from our city who ruled the sidewalks. And when I say sidewalks, I mean all the sidewalks and thoroughfares of the He-Who-Drinks-

73

Water-Is-An-Idiot district. No foreigner could haul her half-naked legs in these parts without incurring our girls' wrath. One must admit in these foreigners' defense that, with our girls, the cost of a trick wasn't within every wallet's reach. Our own girls have a certain way of taking themselves seriously and of thinking their thing is Ali Baba's cave. They even want to be chatted up so they can convince themselves they're not whores in the generally accepted sense.

Where are we going?

In fact, the main street was called At-Least-Six-Hundred-Francs in the old days, before the girls who came from the country over there invaded it and caused a price drop for paid ejaculations, bringing it down, God help me, to one hundred francs only instead of at least six hundred francs! Well then, that spelled early retirement for our Amazons and the *things* they took for Ali Baba's cave. For one hundred francs only, even pedicab drivers could bring their *things* out to thaw. Capitulating in the face of the stamina demonstrated in nail fights by the girls from the country over there, our girls all emigrated to the center of town because over there, apparently, whites don't have time to discuss price. Besides, they set such a high price themselves that even the greatest haggler among our Amazons loses her *Lingala**...

So it is that I know where each hole in the He-Who-Drinks-Water-Is-An-Idiot neighborhood leads, and into which plot I should slip to get to the central thoroughfare that is One-Hundred-Francs-Only Street, formerly At-Least-Six-Hundred-Francs Street, where the hookers who came from the country over there rule as immovable divas.

The story of our neighborhood's name, He-Who-Drinks-Water-Is-An-Idiot, is completely different. In one of

---

* Translator's note: One of Central Africa's national languages.

our languages, *Bembé*, people say: *Ba nwa mamb' biwulu.*
Along with the army of prostitutes at every intersection, it is
in this neighborhood that one counts the greatest number of
watering holes. The population swears by beer, red wine or
palm wine only. Drunkenness contests are held often. People
empty a bottle of palm wine by holding it between their
teeth, without the help of their hands. In these conditions,
he who drinks water really is an idiot. The song by Zao,
"Everyone calls me a drunkard," is an anthem people break
into here and there:

> *Everyone calls me a drunkard*
> *Me I'm not a drunkard*
> *Me* Ya kopa *me I don't provoke anyone*
> *Red wine has reddened my eyes*
> *I am only waiting for death*
> *Palm wine has reddened my lips*
> *I am only waiting for a fight*
> …
> Waï, *me I'm having my drink*
> Waï, *why are you provoking me*
> Waï, *me I'm having my drink*
> Waï, *me I don't want a fight*
> Waï, *me I'm having my drink*
> Waï, *me I don't want to box*
> Waï, *me I'm having a drink*
> *Why are you against me…*

If this woman in white I had glimpsed in the semidarkness
was a streetwalker, as I believed, she had to be new to the
neighborhood. So she had finished her work and was
waiting for a taxi. However, at this time of day, you have to

be prepared to wait for more than forty-five minutes before you can secure a means of transportation. Taxicabs prefer the center of town, where rides are more lucrative and clients less grumpy. Meters are mandatory in the center of town, whereas in working-class districts clients and cab drivers insult each other until they eventually settle on a price, each remaining convinced that the other one screwed him…

I got closer to the girl and told her I was an unlicensed cab driver. This doesn't come as a surprise to anyone in our town, where taxis that aren't real taxis are more plentiful.

She made as if she were going. Well, shit, I exclaimed, where was she going to run to in this dark night, where you couldn't see past your own nose? And what's more, was she aware that I knew this neighborhood and that, even without Angoualima's legendary shoes, I could run in the direction opposite to hers and catch up with her in a flash just a few streets away?

Good. She understood that fleeing would be no use. There she was, defying me with her tall stature. Indeed, I came up to her shoulders. Her gaze filled with mistrust, she asked me where my vehicle was. I pointed toward a direction in the darkness.

"Ah, no, I'm not going over there. Bring your taxi over here!"

"But, madame, we people have to juggle to earn a living. What if the police were hiding somewhere?"

"That's really not my problem!"

"Madame, you yourself must understand, I haven't gotten a ride since this morning and I have to feed a wife and five children…"

I pretended to be tearing up. She hesitated a few seconds, made up her mind, and held her purse tightly under her armpit.

"Okay, let's go fast. I'm very much in a hurry as you see me here."

"Very well, let's go," I said, finding it difficult to mask my euphoria.

I congratulated myself on playing my part well. I hadn't drawn too near, so she had not perceived the alcohol that made my head spin a little. She was right behind me, two or three steps away. I tried to walk without staggering, and that wasn't easy with several glasses of gin in my blood. It must have been ten or ten-thirty at night. A smell of rot from the stream that cuts our city in two was floating in the light nocturnal breeze.

I quickened my pace, the girl did too, and I heard her women's heels crush the rubble behind me. Deep down, I was now hesitating and didn't know which alley to take.

I silenced the thoughts that were going through my head because the moment you must act, especially at night, is no time to act like a philosopher of the Enlightenment.

However, some questions came back to me. How could she have swallowed my story? Did I look like a cab driver, me, the sheet-iron and auto-body professional? When had this girl begun to invade our sidewalks, here in He-Who-Drinks-Water-Is-An-Idiot? Why was she ending her work at this hour if she knew she didn't have a car or a deal with a pimp with wheels, like the other girls did?

Me, a cab driver? You could die laughing! It's true that gypsy cab drivers are so poorly put together that it's easy to establish a general picture of them. They look like any flashy neighborhood interloper. They don't wash and they stink of sweat. They have these cars: I can't even begin to tell you. You have to be a genius just to get them to start.

Between us, I don't mind looking like an unlicensed cab driver. Why not? Like them, I am not handsome, although I am far from being as repulsive as the Great Master Angoualima was when he was discovered on the wild coast, in the middle of a circle, arms crossed. Still, I do not experience my ugliness as despair. I have adapted to it to the point that I now feel a deep love for myself and even consider it is other people who are ugly. I have nothing to regret about my external appearance. Why wouldn't I have the right to love myself? Why wouldn't I be satisfied with my appearance, even if it is unattractive?

I hate beautiful beings because they have done nothing to deserve it and because it's society that decrees they are beautiful. Imagine a world where the ugly were in fact those we deemed beautiful and where people like us would be considered Adonises! Beauty is a value, and values only have the force that we accord them. This is why I have reason to console myself. This being said with complete humility, what I especially appreciate about myself is the fact that people listen to me and trust me right away, like this woman in white. She was hostile at first and then, all of a sudden, she was in. This particular strength is innate, and no one can take it away from me. Being good at making contact is an important skill in life.

You will tell me that all this belongs in the realm of psychology only. Yes, but personally, when I am speaking about myself, this being said with complete humility once again, I'd rather look in this direction than dwell on the physical aspect, to which I can add nothing because I do not share society's values. In society's eyes, I am not tall, I have a rectangular head, I have a big nose, I have small eyes, I have skin that car grease has made all the blacker. Is anyone forgetting that my hands, while large, accomplish miracles when I tackle damaged vehicles? Never has any one of my clients complained to me afterwards. At most, crumbling under too much work, I am often compelled to turn down certain repairs, even for the most important characters in our city, no matter what tip they might wave in front of my nose. Okay, that's not the point, I know…

So the girl in white was behind me. After One-Hundred-Francs-Only Street, she suddenly stopped.

"What are you doing here? Where's your taxi, huh? You're going around the neighborhood in circles!"

"Take it easy, sister, I parked it just over in the next street, we're here. It's a red Renault 19."

"Don't call me your sister, we don't know each other! And what's more, I don't see your Renault there!"

I didn't want to argue, being of the opinion that we didn't have the same IQ. If I had sought to elevate the level of our discussion, the girl would have gotten lost in the tortuous paths of her ignorance, I was sure of it. This being said with complete humility, I do have enough intellectual ammunition to disarm more than a few, and I keep it in reserve for worthwhile encounters.

So now whores have started reasoning as well? Where are we going? I said to myself.

I kept on walking. The girl mumbled insults but eventually followed me. We took Daddy-Happiness-It's-Me Street and reached Heads-of-Negroes Street, which is in fact a sort of public dump in spite of the many signs saying:

PUBLIC LITTERING IS PUNISHABLE BY A FINE

Young people given to provocation had changed the word *fine* to *line*.

In Heads-of-Negroes Street, the population defecates

everywhere, by day as by night, especially in the stream that cuts the city in two and that our current mayor, in order to win the election hands down two years ago, baptized the "Seine" with much fanfare of drums and maracas. He explained to the inhabitants that the real Seine, in France, also cuts the city of Paris in two: on one side is the left bank, on the other the right bank. I won't even try to explain our mayor's gift for persuasion, for galvanizing crowds just like in our animistic churches. He had us understand that it was more than an honor for us to identify ourselves with this dream city, so that we would feel as if we were in Paris, and that it was not given to any ordinary third-world country to have the chance to have a body of water cutting one of its urban areas in two. Did we truly realize how lucky we were, we folks who didn't see what was happening elsewhere, we folks who believed that this stream went through the city as a result of hydrographical circumstances, we folks who didn't know how to profit from the advantages that nature had presented us with, and so on and so forth, he had argued during his election campaign's last meeting. And he was elected right away in the first round, having promised us—a promise unfulfilled to this day—that the mayor of Paris, his personal friend, he assured us, with whom he talked on the phone every week, would come visit…

As I was saying, our city has this specific character, with this stream, I mean with this "Seine" that cuts it in two. People on the Right Bank live on a slightly raised ridge whereas the other group, of which I am part, is crowded together lower down, on the Left Bank, where the "Seine" comes to die—with excrement wrapped in little baggies arriving for the most part from the Right Bank, even though the people who live there are said to be very civilized because they are not very far from the center of town…

On the Left Bank, skeletal dogs fornicate along the banks of this stream where colonies of excited toads make their home. On the Left Bank, still, where the most populated neighborhood is He-Who-Drinks-Water-Is-An-Idiot, water puddles do not dry out. Me, I live over near the last dwellings, in a concrete house that I built with my own hands, as I like to say over and over again. In the other half of my plot is a huge shed that serves as my sheet-iron and auto-body shop.

"Are you on the Left Bank or the Right Bank," I asked the girl.

"What's your problem?" she answered.

"Well, I'm just asking, just to chat while waiting to…"

"What do you mean, aren't we there yet? I have no desire to chat with you!"

"I only want to know where you…"

"What are you, a cab driver or a cop, huh?"

"Sister, I think that you yourself…"

"Don't call me your sister, I said!"

"You must have problems."

"Me? I have problems? Me? Is it any of your business? What's more you stink of alcohol!" she barked at me at the end of Heads-of-Negroes Street.

There was no way to have a conversation with her. Right away I thought she was too haughty and well deserved the death I was planning for her. To dare speak to me like that, to me? To mention cops, people I abhor with the same animosity Angoualima bore them?

She herself was now giving me reasons to hasten my gesture. If she'd at least shown some courtesy, I might have let myself be softened, I would have listened to the echo of human feelings and tempered my determination. However, that wasn't the case. I believed that I was right to shut her up, to teach her how to speak to people she didn't know. A girl is hanging around in the street at an hour when taxis are nowhere to be found, a Good Samaritan offers to take her back home, a Good Samaritan who bravely faces police controls, and this girl, she thinks she is a neighborhood queen and insults her savior, saying "You stink of alcohol!" Wasn't this an attitude that would justify the final punishment awaiting her?

Things deteriorated more and more because I started to laugh.

"Why are you laughing like that, you're a real idiot, you are!"

"Is it now forbidden to laugh, sister?"

"I'm not your sister!"

"I try to be nice and…"

"You're just a drunk, and I'm not about to get into your rotten cab!"

"What kind of language is that, sister?"

"I told you not to call me your sister, you can't hear or what?"

"And so you say I'm an idiot, a drunk, is that it?"

"Yes, an idiot, a real neighborhood drunk! And in which watering hole is it that you have membership, huh?"

Oh, shit! Me, an idiot? Me, a drunk? Me, having *membership* in a watering hole? My cab was rotten? Had she even seen it, this whore washed up in the last tide from the country over there? And what else now?

The farce had lasted long enough. I raised my voice to set things straight and keep a female lacking in IQ from becoming arrogant.

"That's enough now, idiot! Follow me and shut your mouth, which stinks more than the alcohol I drank."

"It's your own mouth that stinks, you drunk! Look at

your head—what is that, a brick?"

"I told you to shut your mouth, you dirty whore!"

"Me, a whore? Did you take a good look at me, huh? Poor bastard, get to your taxi by yourself!"

She turned around and started heading back in great strides. I ran and caught her left hand. Feeling like she was about to scream, with all my strength I slapped her face with the back of my hand. She resisted anyway, the bitch, and although I wasn't expecting it, swung her purse into my face while letting out a howl from deep inside her throat.

Well shit, what did she imagine? That she was going to escape? That I was going to let go? *If that's the way it's going to be, we'll see what happens*, I told myself.

I tackled her like I used to do in football when I was a kid and had to destroy the opponent who had ventured into our penalty area. She didn't realize at what moment her feet left the ground and found herself in a sitting position, a bit dazed. I was behind her, trying to figure out how to immobilize her before she pulled herself back together. I grabbed a piece of dead wood that was lying on the ground. Oh, shit. I gave a sharp blow to the nape of her neck and saw her eyes roll back into their sockets. She passed out completely, legs and arms wide apart, calling her mother for help.

I tore her flowery top, then her long skirt, its endless buttons popping one after the other. Then I moved on to her lace underwear, which was also white.

She was naked now.

I spread her legs wider apart and then I let my denim overalls drop to my ankles. I was breathing like a buffalo that's short of breath. I almost tore my underpants. I felt fire in my lungs, but also at the level of my testicles, like when I caught a glimpse of notary–real estate agent Fernandes Quiroga's young mistress's behind.

Yes, the girl in white was there, in front of me. Was I to have her on the spot? No, you had to be careful not to ruin a good thing.

I turned her immobile body over to admire her frame loaded with goodies. That was it: I wanted to start by taking her by the frame, then I would see what would come to mind later. But no, I had to empty myself on her face, so that she'd wake up later with a coagulated puree that she would remember all her life, even if she washed her face with bleach. Yes, I was going to take her like this, and in such a bestial manner that I'd make her ovaries burst and her tubes turn inside out!

Oh, shit. I didn't understand why I could no longer, like any normal man, get a hard-on while looking at her chest endowed with two enormous watermelons, at her flat stomach, at her barely visible belly button, and her long and firm thighs.

Okay. I had to go about it another way and not get discouraged. The solution was simple. I had to arouse myself with saliva.

I spat into my hands several times and started touching my *thing* gently at first, then frantically, eyes closed, while thinking about the district's most appetizing hookers.

Nothing doing. My *thing* contracted and resembled a premie's. I resented my idol with his twelve fingers. How on earth did this genius manage to get his big *thing* going at the right moment? Had he been faced with a breakdown similar to the one I was experiencing?

All that thinking about him was perhaps getting me farther away from the likelihood of getting my own *thing* going. I felt humiliated and couldn't explain this disappointment to myself. I was a good-for-nothing after all, and I restrained myself from crushing my testicles.

I now found the woman's sunken body in front of me exasperating. I was tingling from stroking my thing with my large workman's hands. My scrotum, which had doubled in size, seemed to have risen up into the lower part of my abdomen.

I had to try something else again. I am stubborn. In case of a breakdown, thank God, a blow job is the male's last buoy. The girl was not in a condition to do it for me? She was unconscious? Well, I was going to do it myself, of course. I kneeled down to slip my disobedient *thing* in her mouth, telling myself that the warmth of the girl's lips and tongue would awaken a trace of desire in me. I wasn't mistaken about that, as my *thing* began to nod its head like a grey lizard stirred from its torpor.

It was about time, I told myself, opening my eyes...

At this very moment I noticed two blinding lights in the distance. A car was going to drive by. It could only come toward us because on the other side was the fetid stream, the "Seine" that had allowed our eloquent mayor to be elected with Stalinist numbers, so much so that for the next election his opponents had already thought of naming this same stream, in their turn, "The River of Love"! You don't change an election tactic that's already led to victory.

With the car not very far from us, my *thing*, disconnected from reality and indifferent to the emergency, surprised me by hardening to the point that it was brushing up against my navel. I wasn't able to get my clothes back on because it had straightened out so fully and was refusing to retreat before I used it. I nearly maimed myself while pulling up my overalls with great force.

The girl coughed lightly several times.

She was going to come to in the next few minutes. I vanished behind the houses nearby. I went through two or three lots, climbed lantana hedges without fearing the barbed wire or the barking packs of neighborhood dogs. I was running like a madman, breathless with alcohol.

When I reached One-Hundred-Francs-Only Street, a taxi with a beat-up frame, which would have deserved my professional care, was waiting, I have no idea whom for. I forced the door open and rushed inside while the cab driver, stirred from his sleep, stared in amazement…

Twenty minutes later, the taxi stopped in front of my house. I paid for the ride and pushed my plot's bamboo gate.

I headed straight for my workshop. I had a few wounds on my arms. They weren't so important that I needed to tend to them that night.

I slept in a damaged car that belonged to one of my latest clients, a retired customs officer who'd become a clerk in charge of renting market stalls at He-Who-Drinks-Water-Is-An-Idiot's Great Market…

2.

I now know what went wrong with the girl in white. Sure, random murder exists, but I don't believe in it. In order to succeed you need willpower as well as, I will repeat it, preparedness. Except, of course, if you demonstrate an exceptional gift like my idol Angoualima.

Take that day, for one, and it annoys me so much that I can't stop blaming myself when I think back on it! Try as I might, day in and day out, to see what didn't work out, I still can't forgive myself for my behavior at the time.

I have been talking in a choppy, almost winded manner since then, and without stopping. I talk to myself as I usually do, which is to say confusedly and with this vulgarity that, contrary to the education I received here and there in the wealthy families, attests to my street culture, the one in which I feel most comfortable.

This is what I whisper to myself, more or less: *what an idiot I was, I let myself get screwed like a greenhorn,* yes, how can I explain to myself that, on that night, I left Take and Drink, This Is The Cup Of My Blood late, I told myself that I was just going to have a bit of a stroll in the heart of He-Who-Drinks-Water-Is-An-Idiot to start on my way, on my consecration as unquestioned disciple of Angoualima, and I crossed paths with this woman I took for a whore and who in fact wasn't one, and since I believed that she in fact was one the timing was perfect, well fuck, I had to kill her because I had to kill someone that very night, I'd had enough with postponing till tomorrow what I could have accomplished that instant, and even if this impertinent and haughty girl was not really a whore, tell me then, she shouldn't have been waiting for her taxi at the spot where Left Bankers know it's always whores walking around there, so it was perfect timing for me, so it was bad timing for her, seeing that, as I had told Angoualima on his grave one day, I had sworn to myself that I was going to clean up He-Who-Drinks-Water-Is-An-Idiot, that I was going to clean it up real good, give it back some dignity, rid it of its refuse, of its detritus, of its filth, of its germs, of its amoebas, of its bacilli, yes of its bitches who came from the country over there, its bitches who disloyally compete with our own girls, I hate these bitches because they sell off their tired attributes like secondhand chewing gum, I hate them because they sell them off to the despairing, to poor bastards lacking in affection who come out of watering holes called Drinking Makes You Hard, Take And Drink, This Is the Cup of My Blood, You Break Your Glass You Buy It, This Place Is Home, Drink And Pay Tomorrow, No Problem We'll Worry About It Later, Even The President Drinks, and I happened to be coming out of Take And Drink, This Is The Cup of My Blood, this watering hole where I am one of the most highly-thought-of regulars because I'm always the one fixing the owner's car when he puts a dent in it, and so I can drink entire bottles of gin on the house, what do you think, well fuck, and on that night I was convinced that I was going to kill at last, crush, wipe out, I don't give a fuck about words, that I was going to exist at last, that's it, exist, that I was going to be somebody, that I was going to follow in Angoualima's footsteps, come out of the banality of my life as a poor sheet-iron man, a poor auto-body man with large hands, as a good-for-nothing, as a man who does the rounds of He-Who-Drinks-Water-Is-An-Idiot's watering holes, that I was finally going to hear the national press and the press of the country over there wonder who this new Angoualima was, who is this murderer, how far will he go, why did he kill a hooker not far from the "Seine," is he a pimp, is he her husband, is he a family member, these are all the questions that make the criminal's popularity ratings go up, and well fuck, on that night it was my day, my own day, my own day just for me, who else would have stolen it from me, what other criminal would have stolen the spotlight on the same day at the same time, well fuck, this was really my day, the day I would finally see the still-warm corpse of my first whore at my feet, I would have been the happiest man on earth, I would have forgotten all the little jobs of times past, the pierced eye of the traitor brother, Master Fernandes

Quiroga's smashed skull, the stolen cars, the wallets belonging to invalid, bed-ridden seniors, I would have forgotten all that because I would have been buoyed by a more sublime gesture, crowned from one day to the next, well fuck, like an imbecile, like a virgin, like a greenhorn, I let myself go, I let myself diverge from my plan, my strategy, my main objective, I told myself that Angoualima always used his big *thing*, his "fifth limb" as muscular as Mayi River fishermen, that he left twenty-five cigars in his female victims' *things*, and why not, yes, why not me, sure I didn't have any Cuban cigars, sure my *thing* was not as huge as my idol Angoualima's, sure, sure again, sure always and always again, but with these sures how do you figure we'll get anywhere, move forward, understand that every one of us has his own fingering, his trademark, as the Great Master of crime himself told me at the cemetery of The-Dead-Who-Are-Not-Allowed-To-Sleep, if this goes on I will go crazy, I will lose my head, I will walk naked into the streets of He-Who-Drinks-Water-Is-An-Idiot, I am capable of it, and well shit, on that night, even without a *thing* as big as my idol's, I could still have made the symbolic gesture, knocked this bitch out, taught her to respect my neighborhood's alleys, this neighborhood where I spent my childhood, this neighborhood that's my mother, this neighborhood that's my father, this is where I played rag-ball, this is where I've always burrowed, this is my own neighborhood, this neighborhood that I know better than any Left Banker, this neighborhood that has become the entire country's shame, and understand me, how can I stand it that the country over there points its finger at us as if it weren't its own whores who tarnished the reputation of our urban area, these whores who arrive in our city in their canoes as if we were still in the time of the Gold Rush, for them this is Peru, this is Eldorado, these whores settle here like ordinary citizens, they blend into the masses neither seen nor known, they speak our languages, they go into our hospitals, they use our public transportation, they eat our food, they dress like our girls, and what's more they're more beautiful than our girls, and what's more they do it better, and what's more everybody knows they do it better but no one dares raise their voice, they do it better because they've been practicing since adolescence with their parents' complicity, they do it better because they know where to put their hands, where to put their mouths to make us glide like paper planes, and you want me to cross my arms when these people over there dare lecture us on TV, on the radio, in the newspapers, they say that we're lying because it's not their girls who are whoring in our country but our own girls who are concealing their shameful activity, whose profits are nevertheless taxable, so people over there say that it's our own girls who are trying to pass as their own girls, I mean, you think that with such an affront, at the time when Angoualima was still Angoualima, at the time when it was still worth committing a crime, you think things would have happened in this manner, you think that, at the time, my idol would have let these blasphemous remarks go without response, without reprisals, where are we going here, well fuck, given that people from the country over there doggedly maintain to the bitter end that it's not their own girls who are whoring here and that it is ours who are doing it, I, Grégoire Nakobomayo, I am taking these people from the country over there at their word, and I am going to wipe out these hookers one after the other, and we will see if they are buried in our country or expatriated in their canoes to the country over there, their true country of origin, for the corpse, whore or no whore, must indeed return to its native ground, because the fruit must rot at the foot of the tree that bore it and not the other tree, we shall see indeed what is going to happen, that's it, and so I made up my mind, I had to kill this impertinent girl in white who had dared criticize my rectangular head, who had dared tell me that I stank of alcohol, that my breath smelled of licorice, she may not have said it this way, with this very beautiful word, but for me it's the same thing, she'd also said, listen to this, that my cab, which doesn't even exist, was rotten, and so on and so forth, and me, instead of going straight to the point, instead of killing her nice and neat, suddenly there was this idiotic desire to ride her frontally, to understand what the Great Master Angoualima felt when he raped his victims with his size XXXL *thing* and stuck his twenty-five Cuban cigars in a woman's strategic spot, this strategic spot that remained gaping for months because my idol wrecked all the natural rubber fibers that allow the woman's *thing* to assume once again a serene air, an innocent face, the face of one who has never done anything serious, the face of one who has never cheated on anyone, the face of one who makes you believe that you're the only one she does it with, so there was this desire that burned my lower abdomen, this desire to see the girl in white's frame loaded with goodies, this desire to paw her two watermelons that had become cheaper at my feet, this desire to smear her everywhere, on her stomach, feet, thighs, watermelons, face, this desire to leave her my coagulated puree as a signature, this was the only way I could sign my gesture, still lacking a short and efficient nickname like Angoualima, whose name kept the police from closing their eyes, so I had to knock her down on the spot, and lo and behold my *thing*, which had always obeyed me until that night, unexpectedly indulged in contracting, rebelling, prancing, having an attack of nerves, refusing to stand at attention, and me in all this what do I do, yes what do I do, I could not rape the girl with a *thing* as soft as a *Bateke* palm tree caterpillar, so in any case it's okay buddy, I am going to follow through with my plan, killing this girl who had the audacity to swing a purse in my face that may not have been a Chanel, that may not have been a Gucci, that may not have been a Vuitton, but certainly one of those bags in fake crocodile skin, fake lizard skin, fake anaconda skin that the Great Market's shoemakers sell, and I guarantee you that a fake bag like that, a bag for the non-bourgeois, always hurts your face really bad, so the objective was to kill this girl who had insulted me and there is no nobler reason to kill than to avenge an insult, Angoualima himself couldn't stand insult and that's why he decided to wipe out the city's bandits who claimed they were the real Angoualima, so this girl had insulted me, and insult, you know this as well as I do, it used to cost dearly in centuries past, it even seems that people set things straight in duels, that they found themselves missing an eye, that they killed each other for it, it even seems that people went to war to win back their honor, their pride, well fuck, she had insulted me, the bitch, it was more than reason enough, I had to kill her to wash away this disgrace, because what would happen then if from now on you let whores from the country over there spit on people from over here who could be their potential clients, you give these girls this much and they want more, but listen up, would the people from the country over there cross the Mayi River in canoes just to have three minutes' paid ejaculations in our country, when, we are told every day, there are plenty of girls over there, so you see I had to kill her, this girl in white, so that she wouldn't open her mouth that stank more than the gin I drink, so that she would no longer deliver her insults to real Left Bankers like me, but then why didn't I succeed, yes, why, well, because it was complicated, yes, I am an imbecile, all I had to do was tell myself that if only I had once again picked up the piece of dead wood with which I had knocked her down after tackling her like the time when, in my youth, I played football and, this being said with complete humility, I played formidable defense in the penalty area, if only I had kept on hitting the nape of her neck with this dead tree, I would have obtained an acceptable result, at least she would have been dead before the arrival of this damned vehicle that screwed everything up, and me, my only solution was to scurry off like a rat, I am ashamed of what the great maestro Angoualima might have thought in his grave if he saw me sneaking in and out of plots, exasperating packs of dogs, getting caught in barbed-wire traps and climbing lantana hedges, because he, Angoualima, had never scurried off and had remained master of the situation, and that's why I told myself, the day after this bitter failure, that I had to go and seek his forgiveness in front of his grave at the first hour, to ask him for advice since, even dead, my idol listens to the prayers of those who follow in his footsteps, so I gave up on beginning the repair on one of my latest clients' cars, this former customs agent who had become a clerk in charge of renting market stalls at He-Who-Drinks-Water-Is-An-Idiot's Great Market, in no time I made my way to the cemetery of The-Dead-Who-Are-Not-Allowed-To-Sleep, on the other side of town, where the "Seine" narrows more and more until it loses itself in a mess of ferns, this cemetery being designed to bury people the government decrees are the most dangerous in the country, and we know for these people there is no funeral procession, no flowers, there are no songs by old women, there's no funeral oration, these people, they are buried at dawn, with complete discretion, you can visit them, but after a long ID check and after justifying your family relationship with them, so the day after my failure to murder the girl in white I successfully started the carcass of the Peugeot 404 the former customs-agent-turned-market-stall-agent had left me, and I assure you his vehicle braked when you wanted to accelerate and accelerated when you wanted to brake, fortunately I was an expert and was able to thwart the old jalopy's whims by making it believe that I was going to brake when in fact I was accelerating, and that I was going to accelerate when in fact I wanted to brake, and that's how I managed, and to think that in a normal car I would have gotten there in a half hour, with my former customs-agent-turned-market-stall-agent's car I arrived at the cemetery of The-Dead-Who-Are-Not-Allowed-To-Sleep an hour later, that's right, and on that morning the groundskeepers must have thought they were dreaming or that I was just a ghost returning to its grave after spending all night scaring children who, instead of doing their homework, loiter in the alleys, steal papayas, steal mangoes, steal tangerines, steal grapefruits, and that's why the groundskeepers looked at me with sympathy and commiseration, then let me through without asking too many questions, they said nothing, they went on with their morning snooze I fought to immobilize the Peugeot's carcass near the first graves, then I walked along a lane of acacias, my hurried step disturbing the crows chatting in patois on the crosses of nearby graves, and it's not by chance that Angoualima was buried at the other end of the cemetery, he had to be isolated at all costs, he had to be watched over from afar, because his resurrection is expected, we in this city all know that Angoualima's grave is a mound of dirt with a ridiculous wooden cross, that it is the most visited in the cemetery and you can distinguish it by the number of cigarette butts, of joints thrown here and there, that only his name and the date of his death are on there because no one knows his birth date, and me, I stopped in front of the mound of dirt, and, since I only smoke Camels, well, I lit one up and threw it on the grave, I didn't have any marijuana, that would have made him happier than a Camel, and I kneeled down, eyes closed, I wanted to talk, explain to him in detail what happened, but my mouth seemed sewn up and my tongue caught between my teeth, my heart was beating so hard I told myself I was going to collapse on the grave, and me, instead of speaking, I once again saw the actions of the day before, scene after scene, and I was convinced, as I am every time I make my way to this grave, that Angoualima was listening to me, and I wasn't mistaken because after a while, there was this fog that I knew now, that at first I took for an illusion, oh shit, lo and behold the Great Master appeared before me, Imperial, Divine, Colossal, Powerful, Sublime, equal to himself, seated on the mound of dirt, legs together, and I saw his twelve fingers, and I saw his head bulging in the back, and I saw his bushy eyebrows, and I saw his old ram's goatee, and I saw his harelip, and I saw the scars on his face, but I immediately lowered my gaze, this mythical character, this charismatic character is none other than my own God and consequently you don't return God's gaze, you are content with believing Him to be alive, eternal, unchangeable, omniscient, you tell yourself that He is the beginning and the end of time, therefore you grovel, you put knee to earth, you cross your hands, you agree with every word, that's what I did, I tried to hold back my sobs, and the Great Master started speaking to me like he's always spoken to me, perhaps also like he speaks to all the shady characters in our city who come beg for his benediction, for his mentoring for their next criminal acts:

"*What is it now, Rectangular Head, are you bringing me good news or not?*" he said.

"Great Master, I must talk to you, it's very important," I answered.

"*Ah, here we go! When am I going to rest at last and not be disturbed by your wailing?*"

"Great Master, you are everything to me."

"*You are not doing anything to convince me of your faith!*"

"I do my best, Great Master, and you know it, you who see everything…"

"*This is unbelievable, really! You are the one who visits me the most and yet you are the least gifted!*"

"Great Master, I made a mistake and I've come to confess…"

"*This is not your first, let me remind you!*"

"I am just an imbecile, Great Master."

"*That goes without saying! I am relieved that you are now aware of it, which saves me wasting my breath.*"

"I don't understand what happened to me last night, Great Master."

"*You don't understand anything that is happening to you anyway!*"

"Yet I was just one hair's breadth away from my first murder, Great Master."

"*And so you come and disturb me for a failure! When will it be for some real news?*"

"It's going to be soon. I've had enough, Great Master, plus…"

"*What, are you crying like last time?*"

"I can't help it, Great Master…"

"*Imbecile, what do you want me to do, huh? Go kill in your stead? Is that it?*"

"Great Master, the truth is that in this case I…"

"Don't count on me!"

"I would like to remind you that…"

"Speak fast, I don't have time to devote to you like last time, when you told me about your little car theft."

"I want to be your disciple, Great Master, it is for this reason that I do all this…"

"Ahaha! He is not yet born who will come up to my heel, if that!"

"I agree, Great Master, you are without equal…"

"You think I am blind below this dirt?"

"No, Great Master, I wouldn't dare think that."

"You think I am the type to let myself be eaten up by worms?"

"No, Great Master, I wouldn't dare think of that."

"You know that from here I saw what you did yesterday in the He-Who-Drinks-Water-Is-An-Idiot neighborhood?"

"Yes, great Master, we all know that you see everything…"

"I see everything how… ?"

"Yes, like the eye of Cain, Great Master."

"That's good. You've learned your lesson."

"Thank you very much, Great Master."

"Let's go back to your deed last night. Are you proud of yourself?"

"No, Great Master…"

"Is this how a true criminal behaves himself?"

"No, Great Master…"

"Is this how I would have acted?"

"No, Great Master…"

"Stop repeating 'Great Master' like a parrot, it is really starting to get on my nerves!"

"Yes, Great Master…"

"Imbecile! You brought disgrace to a profession I made this city respect."

"Great Master, the fact of the matter is I had too much to drink, but what must I do now?"

"Who is the killer? Is it you or me?"

"It's me, Great Master…"

"Therefore, it is for you to know when, how and where, is this perfectly clear?"

"Great Master, your experience is…"

"Ah, that's just how I picture stupidity! Every criminal has his manner of killing, and it is not by aping what I accomplished that you will get people talking about you. As I do for all those who come here, I will repeat to you that there was and there will be only one Angoualima in this country, is that clear?"

"It's very clear, Great Master, you are our example, our guide and…"

"You are nothing but a pathetic character!"

"Great Master…"

"Yes, a pathetic character!"

"Great Master, if you will allow me, you congratulated me once when I told you about the assault on my adoptive brother, his eye that I had…"

"Yes, but you didn't kill him, this scion of the wealthy, so why bother me with that?"

"I was young, I was taking my first steps, Great Master!"

"There's no good age to be a fool, you've proved it!"

"Great Master…"

"There was just one time I was proud of you, that's all, I don't see any other occasion."

"Yes, Great Master?"

"One time only, and I told you so: You took up my defense on the program Listeners Speak Out. *From where I was hiding I told myself, what nerve, this young man has a future! Alas, I was wrong."*

"Great Master, you congratulated me nevertheless…"

"And so what? Is this what makes you think I've handed you the torch of crime in this shitty city?"

"No, Great Master…"

"I allowed you to address me casually in front of my grave. As a matter of fact you are the only one who has this right. That was to thank you for your intervention in Listeners Speak Out. *That's not enough for you?"*

"It suits me, Great Master…"

"Now we're even, Rectangular Head!"

"Great Master, I can't stand it when people disrespect you, when I think that like me you were a picked-up child and I…"

"Shut up, imbecile! You think you now have the right to call me a picked-up child because we are on familiar terms?"

"I wouldn't allow myself, Great Master."

"What do you yourself know about it?"

"Nothing, Great Master…"

"You weren't even born when I was young, so don't go spreading what the street says about me!"

"I wouldn't allow myself, Great Master…"

"Was it you who crossed the Mayi River to reach the country over there?"

"No Great Master."

"Do you even know how things work in the other country?"

"No, Great Master."

"Do you know how the old bandits from over there gave me their powers?"

"No, Great Master."

"'Picked-up child!' I don't like this term!"

"Neither do I, Great Master, I don't like this term, which…"

"In any case, wasn't Moses picked up somewhere?"

"He was picked up somewhere, Great Master. He was

even picked up near…"

"Was he called a picked-up child?"

"No, Great Master, he was not called a picked-up child, on the contrary he was…"

"Imbecile! My fate was sketched out for me, well sketched out with a precise objective. And when I understood that I had realized everything and that no one could be my equal, I killed myself to be in communion with those who passed all these powers on to me. Do you know all this, you?"

"No, Great Master, your story should have been taught in our schools and…"

"So be careful what you say, don't irritate me!"

"Great Master, I apologize for this, it's true people say this, that and the other thing about you, but if you ask me to do so, I can kill all those who take your name in vain. I will kill all the women in this city, my mother included, if somebody would show her to me and…"

"Words! Get some respect for your own name before you start making mine your business. I was very good at getting some respect for my name by myself, I am not expecting anything from anyone."

"No, Great Master, you are not expecting anything from anyone."

"By the way, last time you promised me something, no?"

"What, Great Master? I'm afraid I don't remember."

"Memory is the first quality of a criminal, and you don't have any!"

"Great Master, I beg you…"

"You said you would take a murderer's nickname, so what is it?"

"Great Master I thought something along the lines of Greg the Rattler, Greg the Angry Wasp, Greg Storm, Greg Jack, Greg the Sicilian, Greg Butcher or Greg the…"

"Stop your bullshit! All these names are for laughs! Rectangular

Head would fit you like a glove!"

"Great Master, you are in a better position to give me a name for work…"

"Get out of my sight!"

"Pardon, Great Master?"

"Get out of my sight, I said, you're deaf or what? Lousy good-for-nothing!"

"Great Master…"

"Yes, get out of here! Our conversation is over. From now on stop invoking my name in every circumstance, otherwise I will resuscitate myself just for the pleasure of slicing your throat with a Gillette blade and with the help of my additional fingers. Killing the girl in white from the other night, even a complete amateur could have done it. Now, vanish and come back here when you have some good news to bring me…"

Killing Germaine

1.

I don't put much stock in knives. Anyone can acquire them and know how to use them, more or less. We use them every day and it is almost impossible for mankind to do without them. Would I kill Germaine with such an object? Better to abandon my project than lower myself to that level!

A few days ago, to convince myself that the game wasn't worth the candle with a weapon that had been used even by primitive men, I took a very close look at the broad-bladed knife I had bought at He-Who-Drinks-Water-Is-An-Idiot's Great Market. The salesman guaranteed that it was a unique specimen, used in olden days to cut off in one fell swoop the heads of animals offered in sacrifice to the gods of rain. Truth be told, I bought it more to cut short his chatter than because of the attractiveness of the sharp blade, with which you couldn't even shave your beard. I make no secret of the fact that, having acquired it, I changed my mind and congratulated myself on the purchase, as it had to be used for something. This broad-bladed knife had cost me very dearly, and I wasn't about to peel potatoes with it.

And so it was that I firmly resolved to disembowel Germaine. First, I had to make it so she wouldn't catch sight of the knife when she came back at night. That wasn't a problem: all I had to do was store it away among my work tools, in my workshop. Germaine hardly ever comes into my shed, a place she finds sinister and untidy. I do not share this view. What will she come up with next? Who is she to lecture me? A whore I pulled off the street, talking to me in this manner? Because she thinks the alleyways of He-Who-Drinks-Water-Is-An-Idiot where she cools her heels are cleaner than my shop? A shop I built with my own hands and thanks to my thrift! When you criticize my place of work, you are criticizing me as well, almost insulting me, and I have explained how unbearable insult is to me, how it has driven people to pierce each other's eyes in duels or to launch wars to preserve their honor.

Germaine doesn't understand how I can manage to work in this graveyard for vehicular wrecks and this smell of grease. Do I ask her how she manages to sell her *thing* to people who only take showers in spite of themselves, when it rains? This work is my life. I get my rocks off banging on beat-up cars. I love this untidiness, and I am hostile to neat freaks. To have manias is one thing, but to impose them on others, I can't tolerate! Come on, where are we going? I am trying to be calm, and every time she's the one picking on me and pushing me to get serious...

Since I was planning to use my broad-bladed knife, I arranged to hide it in my shop. All I had to do now was stage the way my deed would unfold. One scenario replaced the other. I tried my hand at stabbing the air, and I heard myself say "No! No!" every time. And so I returned to my gesture, my confidence increased. Still, it wasn't right, because I was acting, and not in the real conditions for the deed. Slightly baffled, I told myself, *we shall see.* I kept on walking, walking up and down the lot.

Never had I racked my brains so much. Angoualima's prophetic words came back to me in an echo. I was going to bring him some good news at last, as he wished, and leave behind the ranks of the pathetic...

Just because you own a weapon doesn't mean that what follows becomes a formality. Where would the crime take place, then? A seemingly stupid question, yet I had two options: in my shed, or else in the house I've been sharing with her since I pulled her off the street and she joined me, apparently because she cannot live without me anymore, because she's in love, because I am a generous human being, sensitive, understanding, altruistic, magnanimous, considerate, blah blah blah. Me, I always laugh deep down inside when I hear people venture blindly into unknown territory. I have noticed that people like us are usually kind because they find it easy to reconcile extreme human feelings. They can become monstrous but also demonstrate a sweetness that would surprise more than a few. I'm like that. Looking at me, you'd think I was a workman like any other, an everyman who earns a living from the sweat of his brow, who pays taxes without flinching, who respects the elderly, who gets his groceries from the Lebanese guy on the corner, who even throws a few coins into the bowls of He-Who-Drinks-Water-Is-An-Idiot's beggars. I believe in our republic, even if I don't vote. I also believe in paper money, in Santa Claus, in man being descended from apes, and all that stuff...

What Germaine doesn't know is that the day I first took her into my house, I was wishing precisely that she settle in as soon as possible, that she build up trust, so I could fatten her up like you fatten a chicken to be eaten during a holiday dinner. I had seen to it that the decision to live with me came from her. That's where she was headed and me, playing my part well, I told her that her work as a whore didn't disturb me, that it wasn't an obstacle, that my mother was a whore too, that whores were the kindest women on earth, that without whores, my God, the world would not be what it is today, that some men wouldn't know what a woman is, that others, frustrated, would sleep with their own mothers or with sheep wandering the neighborhood, that whores were as necessary as notaries, as real estate agents, as ambulance drivers, as plumbers, as sheet-iron or auto-body workers, that I thought politicians should create a department for them because they paid taxes like notaries, like real estate agents, like ambulance drivers, like sheet-iron and auto-body workers, and I saw her smile with her angel face and dimpled cheeks, yes, she kissed me on the mouth and told me again that I was a kind man, a generous man, a magnanimous man, an altruistic man, and so on and so forth. Me, I couldn't give a shit about all this. I fiercely opposed the idea that she stop whoring, which she'd announced while dropping her bag in front of my door.

Please, can you just imagine if she'd stopped whoring?

I had the broad-bladed knife, for sure, but the workshop as crime scene was not doing it for me. How could I possibly ask Germaine, back from her work late at night, to follow me into this sheet-iron shed brimming with vehicular wrecks, burned tires and all kinds of scrap metal? To show her what, exactly, inside it that would justify such eagerness on my part? No, that was no good. I could see her telling me that I thought only about my work, that we'd see tomorrow, and that there was no hurry. Yes, she would do anything not to come into this untidy place. And when Germaine doesn't want to do something, she doesn't budge from her position. I have come to learn this in the few weeks we have lived together.

Germaine is a sensitive girl, romantic, as people say, and you're not going to whisper sweet nothings into her ear in the middle of a scrap heap. As far as she's concerned, she needs candles, flowers, a nice surprise, that's what she told me right from the start. Where she acquired these habits, I don't know. No doubt when she was whoring in the center of town. She told me one day that whites in our town liked to requisition her for the whole night and treat her like you treat a woman you love, and that we, the people of this city, we were barbarians, we went straight for the main course without even marveling at the variety of hors d'oeuvres. The whites in our town, for their part, pop open the champagne, order flowers and serve the girl breakfast in bed. But where are we going? Do you realize that these nuts want to do everything, including, my God, put their mouth on the woman's *thing* though they are aware it's a highway everybody tears through at two hundred kilometers per hour, the only condition being that they wave in the air a large bank note with several zeros for the toll! Do you realize that some whites in our town, God help me, coo things like, *"I love you my pet," "I want you to be mine and only mine tonight, tomorrow night and also the night after tomorrow,"* and like, *"I want you to show me what you can do, what you have never done to anyone else."* And so it may be with these people that Germaine learned these manners, which were really getting to me in the end, when I was riding on her and at every thrust she asked me whether I loved her, and if I did, could I tell her, and if I did, could I not remain mute like this, people can't make love like sheep, I had to talk, say everything that crosses my mind, when in fact I don't like to talk when I'm in the heat of action!

No, I couldn't kill Germaine in my workshop. All that was left was the house. A few weeks living together, and I now knew her habits. She arrived late at night, found me in front of the television, put her purse on a shelf near the entrance and sat down on the sofa-bed while waiting for me to bring her a Heineken.

There was an opportunity, right there. I would not let her sit down on the convertible but have her sit on a chair in the middle of the dining room with lighted candles arranged in a triangle and flowers the way she likes it.

"What's happening?" she would surely say.

"I have a surprise for you," I would answer.

I thought I would blindfold and gag her. The moment she started suspecting something, and therefore started jerking around to try and free herself, it would be too late: I would already have fastened her arms behind her back with cables taken from a moped. Beforehand, even before she came back from work, I would have made the broad-bladed knife red-hot, more than a thousand degrees, in my shop's furnace. It would then be easier to slash her from the place that separates her anus from her *thing* up to her abdomen while holding her legs wide open with cords…

Strengthened by this last idea, one afternoon, after Germaine left, I went through a simulation once again, not wanting to be clumsy when the time came. The mistakes of amateurism were a thing of the past, now was the time to be prepared, even if my first exercises were more discouraging than reassuring.

Entrenched in my shop, I interrupted an urgent and very important repair job: the car belonging to one of the cousins of the mayor of He-Who-Drinks-Water-Is-An-Idiot. I looked closely at the broad-bladed knife I was going to use as murder weapon. I started imagining how the blade would enter Germaine's skin and puncture her intestines. I saw myself driving in even the handle while grinding my teeth. I smiled, because the idea pleased me all of a sudden.

For a long time I talked to myself like I always do. I told myself, in this manner I have of expressing myself before or after dangerous actions: *old chap, here you are now, about to be* crowned, here you are a hair's breadth away from your most important gesture, the one that will leave Angoualima speechless, flabbergasted, aghast, petrified, dumbfounded, yes, old chap, all you will need to do is gather momentum in front of this bound body and drive the broad-bladed knife in with the implacable determination of Sadilleck, the criminal butcher the criminology professor talked about in Listeners Speak Out in the old days, if need be you will repeat the gesture as many times as it gives you pleasure, you will not let yourself be intimidated by the flow of this puddle of warm blood, blood is nothing, it only frightens those who don't like the color red, you yourself don't give a shit, red or not, blood is nothing but a liquid, on the contrary, you will collect it and put it in a bottle and go pour it on Angoualima's grave with the pride of a broken-down horse who's just won a race everybody thought he would lose, yes, you can do it, your large hands are made for this, you must do it, old chap, what are you waiting for, why are you still hesitating, come on, keep on rehearsing it calmly until the scene seems so theatrical to you, so banal, that you could act it out without a weapon, keep at it in empty space like that guy who fought windmills by himself, be mean, show your fangs, roar, growl, implode while thinking solely about your goal, this girl truly deserves punishment with a broad-bladed knife, she had it coming, you've fattened her up enough already, and it may come back to haunt you, as you know full well that when we spend a long time fattening up an animal it ends up becoming familiar, we no longer have the courage to slice off its head, human feelings win over, pity makes the hand heavy, is that what you want, no, tell me that you will go the whole way, that the following day you will run to bring Angoualima the good news at the cemetery of The-Dead-Who-Are-Not-Allowed-To-Sleep, tell me that your idol will applaud you with his hands with twelve fingers, and you will feel your chest swell, you will have become a grownup, a real grownup, come on go for it, keep on rehearsing, old chap...

I proceeded with the second phase of my simulation. I put the broad-bladed knife to redden in the furnace. It was a half hour before I saw the metal glow redder and redder and blend in with the flames. I picked it up with pliers and dipped it in a basin of water. The blade blackened immediately and roared in a blinding cloud of steam. I told myself the object would pierce Germaine's skin with the same noise…

I had become excited. The workshop seemed narrow. I could already see a body lying on the ground, its stomach open. I imagined myself putting it in the trunk of one of my clients' vehicles and driving toward the stream that cuts our city in two. It would be nighttime, the middle of the night, a time when even the neighborhood's prostitutes have left the streets. I would park along the "Seine." I would pull Germaine's body out, hidden in a bag. I would fasten an iron weight to the end of the bag so the body wouldn't come up to the surface once it was in the stream, so that the water would one day take it to the other bank, toward the country over there, so that the fruit would rot at the foot of the tree that bore it…

I swear to you I was a hair's breadth away from going forward with this. Ah, let's say that something convinced me this project would have buried me in ridicule. Every criminal has his pride. What would people have said about this crime? Would it have had the resonance I was hoping for?

No. I couldn't imagine myself in this banal, ordinary scenario fit only for small-time toughs, apprentice criminals. One doesn't enter legend through the back door. Villains on both banks of our neighborhood would have been laughing for months. I would have barely dared to step out of my plot of land. I would have gotten stuck with a nickname like Chicken Little. It was as if I were stabbing my victim in the back. Now, a murder committed from behind does not count for the one who knows how to do things with professionalism. In addition, and this is what I feared most, the police and the courts would have concluded quickly that this was a rape committed by a psychopath. A rape by a psychopath! Words! More words. It's not that being labeled a psychopath would have upset me. It was this rape thing above all. Do you see me raping Germaine, me, after what happened with the girl in white three months ago?

In truth, the reason I did not proceed had to do with a question of principle and even of consideration of the object I was about to use as crime weapon.

Indeed, what revolts me most as far as knives are concerned is the number of murders committed with them. Our city's news items attest to this fact. Only complete imbeciles still operate with this means. More generally, the weapons I place under this heading include: axes, machetes, hoes, *assagai*, paper-cutters like in the Guy des Cars novel, rakes, spades and pickaxes. In addition, in the city, men and women of *Bembé* ethnicity are famous for resorting to knives at the least little thing. The anecdote most often told is one about the referee Kimpolo, an old *Bembé* man nevertheless appreciated for his impartial refereeing of soccer games between the small teams of He-Who-Drinks-Water-Is-An-Idiot. The old man always hides a penknife in the back pocket of his shorts. These games often end in fights in which the man with the whistle is taken to task. Neither team accepts the opposite team's goal, and when the referee says the goal is good, they go after him. Now the inhabitants of He-Who-Drinks-Water-Is-An-Idiot have decreed that knives are *Bembés'* favorite weapons. At it happens, I am not *Bembé*…

Knives? I don't deny their effectiveness. Back when I was still reading, I saw that several famous authors let their characters use them. I am thinking especially of Camus's Arab in The Stranger. Okay, that's another story altogether. It's true that the Arab indeed pulled out his knife, but did he kill the narrator with it? No, it was the narrator, rather, who used a pistol! Better yet, he fired four times on an already inert body!

I also own a chainsaw. As frightful as it may be in and of itself, it makes me think immediately of the movies, of Scarface, a film that played for six months at the Duo, and that I saw twenty-seven times in matinees, thirty-three times in the evening. I watched it from from beginning to end without my eyes ever leaving the screen for one second. I know the dialogue by heart.

However, committing murder is not like acting in a movie.

2.

In the final analysis, it's not that I don't know what I want, but there's something about firearms that bothers me. Why foreshorten the pleasure of killing by shooting your victim in one go? What kind of work is that? Where are we going? Am I such a cretin that I would do that, no matter what my idol Angoualima thinks of me? Would such a method allow me to enjoy a full page in our country's dailies and those of the country over there?

It's true that one of the characteristics of a shot is that it resounds. Except, of course, when the weapon has been equipped with a silencer. All that noise for an operation that could be accomplished another way, without waking the neighbors I neither know nor care to know?

I am convinced that pistols, guns, rifles and all things resembling the above are more interesting to the feeble-minded, the weekend cuckolds or those who want to kill themselves. This being said in complete humility, despite the clumsiness I have demonstrated until now, I am not feeble-minded, I haven't been cheated on by a woman over the weekend and I haven't reached the point where I would kill myself. I love life and I would do anything to keep it, even by being the worst scoundrel on earth, even if it entails dying after a long illness as they say in our radio stations' death announcements, radio stations that can't manage to talk about real facts.

I am in possession of all my faculties and I can tell what is good for me from what isn't. Had my childhood been that of a wealthy scion, I can assure you I would have refused toy guns. I have noticed that, in our city, kids show them off and imagine they're in a movie instead of playing rag-ball like in my childhood. In fact these brats are so ridiculous that it would be preferable if they entertained themselves with their parents' table knives. That would suit them better.

In any case, I don't know who invented the pistol. Probably a coward who had nothing between his legs and feared face-to-face confrontation. Pistols are for chickens. One should be ashamed to use them. The Great Master would share my opinion…

My aversion to firearms may seem paradoxical coming from someone who acknowledges a kinship with the underworld. And so what? I do as I please.

In contrast to the knife, with which you can at least cut up meat that's on the table, as soon as you see a firearm, my God, you know right away that it's meant to kill in the most expeditious manner possible. Bang! Bang! Bang! And that's that. The victim lies on the ground, in a pool of blood, like in detective novels where there's got to be a corpse for an investigation to begin and the murderer to be found in the last pages. I said a few moments ago that committing a crime is not like acting in a movie. Murder is not like writing a detective novel either. What I must accomplish soon is something concrete and more serious than what is being written in fiction to entertain readers, as if the latter had no other occupation than polluting their eyesight with words from stories that aren't even true…

What also throws me, as far as firearms are concerned, is that one of my clients, a former policeman, a nice guy who entrusted his car to me for repairs, told me that the person who takes the bullet doesn't hear the detonation, and that if that person hears it means that he or she isn't dead but just wounded. Okay, I haven't checked all this, but I trust my client, he's handled weapons for years. He doesn't look like he would bullshit me, and in any case, to what end? He's someone who's served the city with devotion and he never misses an opportunity to recite the names of the offenders he put behind bars for a decent period of time. Yes, he's already shot someone. Yes, he's already killed, but he was under cover of the law. He's one of the protected criminals, and they're given a uniform for this, to warn those who think that cops' guns are loaded with blank bullets that such is not the case, that these are real bullets that can kill, to tell these unbelievers that if they are shot there won't be anything after, just like there's nothing after when you put down a rabid pet or a wild beast that's come to disturb the population's peace and quiet. For people in uniform, guys like us are wild animals, rabid beasts to be shot without warning.

That's all.

Consequently, if I am to put an end to Germaine's days with a firearm, I have to get used to the idea that she wouldn't hear the detonation and that the only fear she'd feel would be to see the weapon that I would be pointing in her directions.

It's out of the question of course. I will leave this to gangsters, to armed-robbery specialists from the center of town, and to characters in westerns. These villains think they're the masters of the world just because they can master a firearm.

In truth, I have never touched a pistol, a rifle or a hunting gun. As a matter of fact I don't how these contraptions work.

I guess you have to press somewhere, right at the bottom, in the little space designed for you to slip your index finger. But given my large hands, could my index manage to get into this needle hole? I figure you probably need a long and slender index finger that can get in easily.

Other than that distant night when I caught a glimpse of Master Fernandes Quiroga's gun in a drawer in his office while rummaging through his stuff, the only time I have really seen firearms up close was last week. I wanted to put my mind at ease and quell the doubts that were haunting me as far as the use of such a weapon was concerned. I went to the center of town and stopped in front of the shop of the only gunsmith in our urban area. There were all kinds of weapons there. Some were crafted and had such detail from butt to barrel that I thought the person who died from one of its bullets would go straight to Heaven. Those who manufacture these noisy toys are really consummate sadists. They take days, perhaps entire months, to embellish a tool whose end is killing. Is it the weapon's particular aesthetics or the manner in which the killing is done that gives the criminal gesture, whatever it may be, all of its beauty? Seeing how these Machiavellian manufacturers take pains to overdecorate pistols and guns, I wouldn't be surprised to hear one day that someone had invented poisons that taste like mango or pineapple, poisons that can be bought in a pharmacy upon presentation of a prescription. If you're going to poison someone, you might as well send them into the next world with the sweet taste of death!

I went into the shop out of curiosity. The shopkeeper, a white man with a nose as red as a hot pepper, stared at me for a long time, and I told myself that he had guessed I was getting ready to commit the irrevocable. How can I help you, sir, he asked me, and me, not at all surprised, I answered: I'm just looking, I haven't made up my mind, I don't know anything about this new generation of hunting rifles, I never moved beyond traditional rifles that you load by ramming a rod into the barrel, yes I am a hunter, sir, a great hunter if you want to know, I assure you I have killed elephants as big as buildings, lions as huge as mountains, panthers with double-edged claws, gorillas twice as impressive as King Kong, and I'm not even counting the squirrels I've shot with my eyes closed, do you know, sir, that squirrels are not an easy kill, they're always making faces with an almond in their mouths, yes sir I'd like to change rifles but I'll do that later, for the moment the one I inherited from my grandfather is still working, yes my grandfather was the most renowned hunter in our village, no sir I don't need ammunition, I have plenty, I can even make some like my grandfather used to in the old days, blah, blah, blah.

A man as skinny as a framing nail came in at the same time and asked the shopkeeper if the weapon he had ordered a month ago had arrived. No, it hasn't arrived, if you want I can offer you another one, it's a new shipment, this weapon is all the rage in France, in England, in Papua-New Guinea, thanks to the precision of its aim, its adjustable targeting, its infrared system, it's easy to handle, it's light, it's easy to maintain, see for yourself, what do you mean you only trust a Winchester or a Beretta, you are wrong sir, all this is out of date, you have to follow the evolution of technology, in the old days you had to struggle to load a weapon, now everything's ready in the blink of an eye, all you have to do is aim and shoot, and if I'm not mistaken, even a blind man can use this weapon…

Then I heard them mention something about an

authorization, blah, blah, blah. So in addition, you need to have an authorization in order to own a weapon! Any talk of authorization means registering one's identity somewhere. Why not for knives also? Did our ancestors register their poisonous *assagaï*? Is it the police who want this? So in addition to everything, you have to help these people know who owns what weapon and where that person lives? If I understand correctly, those who are on file are then the first ones to be suspected when a detonation rips through the city? Where are we going?

No, not a firearm. When I think that you need to know how to aim first and not let yourself be frightened by the deflagration, how can I opt for this solution?

I can still remember that Angoualima had stolen weapons and ammunitions from several of this city's precincts. How can we explain that he never used them? It was because the Great Master had an aversion to these weapons. Because he thought they meant utter cowardice. Killing is all well and good, but you have to let your victim at least have the illusion of believing that he'll be able to escape death. With gun a pointed in his direction, what chance would he have? He wouldn't even try to flee anymore, that bullet would catch him in the back.

No, personally, I don't want any of that.

3.

I now know that it's no use looking for the most perfect way to kill Germaine. This is why I have put aside this practical aspect, which was beginning to irritate me. I will kill her eventually. The pleasure I feel when I think that I don't know how I will proceed is beyond all explanation. In fact the question I'm always asking myself is the following:

What death would I not like to suffer myself, should I be so lucky as to be able to choose one?

It is, above all, because I cannot answer this question that I tell myself that what is interesting in death is that, except for those who kill themselves like the Great Master Angoualima, no one can predict what his own will be like. And we are convinced that someone else's death will always be crueler than ours. We hang on to the idea that we will die a nice and quiet death during a sickly sweet sleep, and that the angels will carry us on their wings to Heaven's doors. As a matter of fact, there are periods when the idea of eternity makes its way into our minds. Death seems to us distant and foreign. We tell ourselves that we have time to accomplish everything. And then the hearse driving by, the neighbor's death, the crime we hear about on the radio or read about in the newspaper remind us of our condition as a passenger on Earth...

If I had kept on trying one scenario after another, kept on losing myself in the choice of the appropriate weapon, to this day I would never have made up my mind and would still be postponing my gesture indefinitely. There is a time for reflection. There is a time to get on with it. The main thing is that, when I am face-to-face with her, Germaine suspects nothing. That she settles in the sofa bed, that I serve her a Heineken and ask her how her workday went in the streets of He-Who-Drinks-Water-Is-An-Idiot. Since she is very chatty, I'm sure she will say the same thing. My day went well, darling, I had a lot of work, Sunday is shithead day, and I don't know why but that's the way it is, I got this guy, a so-called head of a corporation, and it was unbearable with his thing breaking down, and me, you know, I swore to you on my mother's and on my father's graves in the country over there, yes I swore to you that I would no longer put my clients' things in my mouth given that I kiss you with the same mouth, I told the old fart this, and he pulled out a wad of new bank notes, so I put a little bit in anyway, but really a tiny little bit of his little thing in my mouth, and you know what, the old fart claimed that I wasn't doing it any better than a girl from Head-of-Negroes Street, that I was hurting him with my teeth, that my head was someplace else, that if this was the way it was going to be he would pay me half price, and me I almost bit his little thing, and so he got dressed, threw the wad of bank notes on the ground, and all evening it was like that, nightmares, clients with problems, actually there was also this other one, I have to talk to you about this one because he's always where I expect him least, I have to talk to you about him, about this railroad ticket collector, pot-bellied, with a toothbrush-shaped mustache, hair coming out of his ears, smelling of sweat, this guy who always calls me all kinds of names, threatens me if I don't bark while he's on me, and today I barked woof! woof! woof! and he said he wanted to hear a real Alsatian or bulldog barking, not a kitten meowing, he slapped me and I screamed, and he came, and he didn't even pay me, the idiot, I'll get him eventually, if I see him again, I'll scratch his face, as a matter of fact I'm going to give his description to my girlfriends, and we'll see if he'll still be able to get any in this neighborhood, we'll put him on the blacklist, yes we have a list for this, we give each other instructions, we tell each other: this one, you can't accept him anymore, this one, you have to send him packing, this one, he has to pay before he even gets undressed, this one, you can't agree to go to his house, yes we have people like that we call "this one," and so this railroad man, we'll tell him to go wipe his ass with his bank notes, we'll all denounce him, and he won't have the courage to show his face, which looks like a guava that's been smashed in the streets, and if he insists, the youth of He-Who-Drinks-Water-Is-An-Idiot will teach him a lesson, I've had it, I'm tired of all this...

She will in turn ask me what I did with my day. Will I answer: *Darling, I forgot to tell you that just a week ago I put a broad-bladed knife in the furnace to kill you tonight, but in the end I found this so ridiculous that I had to give up, and sometime, trust me, I will gratify you with a beautiful death, I am going to free you from your daily troubles, there will no longer be people you call "this one," there won't be any old fart head of a corporation with breakdowns of his thing, or any pot-bellied railroad ticket collector who asks you to bark woof! woof! woof! like an Alsatian or a bulldog, yes I will kill you and don't resent me if up to this day I haven't followed through, it's not easy for everyone, you have to make do with what's close at hand...*

No, I will answer as I usually do. It's easy for a workman to explain how he fills his hours. So I'm not going to beat around the bush. Looking serious, I will say: *I stayed in my workshop, lately I've been so swamped with work that I don't have a minute to myself to smoke a Camel, all clients are tyrants, they break their cars and want them fixed with the wave of a magic wand, what kind of bullshit is this, am I the one telling them to bang up their jalopies, actually, for example this morning, a client brought in a vehicle, or rather what was left of it, that I have to get back into shape in the next two weeks, if you have time, go take a stroll around the workshop, and you'll see the damage, I don't know where to start, apparently it was a serious accident near the Kassaï roundabout, my client was driving at breakneck speed and collided with a parked truck in Mongo-Beti Street, it's a crazy story, he himself doesn't know how he ended up outside the main thoroughfare to crash into a parked vehicle, he got out of it okay, the client, he told me stories about witch doctors, supposedly his uncle is jealous of his car and it's because he got himself good protection by going to a real witch doctor that he got out of it without a scratch, the engine is not damaged too much, and since I dabble in mechanics a little, I'll try and see what I can do for him, but it's going to cost him dearly, I warned him, do you realize that I have to fix the engine first, then do the sheet-iron and even the paint over...*

In short, everyday blather.

4.

I met Germaine a month ago at the Open Air restaurant on the Left Bank. I can still picture to this day the moment I knew she was the one I would kill.

Open Air looks like all the restaurants found in abundance in He-Who-Drinks-Water-Is-An-Idiot: bamboo tables in an immense courtyard stretching to the edge of the street, with old loudspeakers blasting music that can pierce the eardrums of clients and passersby. The smoke clouds the place in general indifference. People scream with laughter, they get up and dance in a corner. Cars park out front and drivers emerge, often accompanied by their latest female conquests.

It was a Sunday afternoon.

I was seated in a corner of the packed establishment, my

gaze a bit distracted. My dish of chicken in peanut sauce was being served at the precise moment I saw Germaine heading toward the cashier's desk. She was talking with the proprietress. It even looked like an argument, for the two women seemed not to agree about something. The proprietress opened an old notebook and showed it to Germaine, who shook her head no. The proprietress closed the notebook and Germaine walked back toward the customers. That's when I finally saw her face. What intrigued me was her somber gaze. She must have had serious problems.

Anyhow, how was this any of my business? So I averted my eyes and focused on cutting the chicken leg that, truth be told, I was finding skinny and tough.

Before I had time to swallow the first bite, Germaine was in front of me.

"Don't you have a cigarette?" she asked me, addressing me casually from the get-go.

To me, her question seemed inane, as my pack of Camels was on the table. I stared at her, this time up close: tall, lightly dressed with her miniskirt and see-through white top, hair pulled back, a round face with dimpled cheeks, and small eyes, deep but dulled by the anxiety that filled her at that moment. I told myself that she was probably one of these whores from the country over there who come to our country in their canoes and whom the shopkeepers of the He-Who-Drinks-Water-Is-An-Idiot district use during the day to incite clients to empty their wallets. I am not criticizing this practice, as I have also occasionally benefited from it. When such was the case, and before Germaine came to live with me, I would find myself with one of these girls at home. But I always took her to my workshop, among the scrap metal on which Germaine was to heap abuse later.

"Help yourself," I answered that day, offering my pack of cigarettes and a lighter.

"You're eating alone?" she continued.

I was now sure she was a whore at night and worked for the restaurant during the day. Why stand on ceremony?

"Take a seat and order what you want," I offered.

"Well, I mean…"

"Take a seat, Germaine."

"How come you know my first name?"

"It's written on the small chain you're wearing around your neck!"

"Ah yes, that's true…"

She pulled up a chair and sat down across from me. Open Air's proprietress, who was keeping a close watch on the scene, immediately sent two of her stork-necked waitresses to prowl around us. They were as excited as flies. Germaine ordered the same dish as mine, with a beer.

"You have great worries, you do," I told her.

"Are you a *marabout* or something?"

"It shows on your face. Is it because of this restaurant's proprietress?"

"No."

"Still, I heard you raise your voices a moment ago!"

"It's not serious, I'm not going to tell everyone my problems."

Her gaze plunged down into her plate.

"I'm not everyone," I shot back. "I can be a good friend, and perhaps I can help you…"

"I don't even know your name!"

"Angoualima…"

"What???"

"My name is Angoualima…"

"No kidding!"

She burst out laughing and finally started eating, then looked me straight in the eyes.

"You joke like that all the time or what?"

"From time to time. It's good to laugh, don't you think?"

"Thank God, Angoualima's dead! In the old days, this head of yours, we would pick it up by the seaside with a Cuban cigar!"

"No, this was just for laughs," I replied.

"So what's your name?"

"My name is Grégoire Nakobomayo, you can call me Greg."

"Greg… Greg… Greg… hmmm… doesn't ring a bell. Do you live in the neighborhood?"

"You could say that. But tell me about your worries instead. I have no appetite when I see a beautiful woman in an awkward position. It is indeed because of the proprietress, wasn't it?"

"I told you it's not, she has nothing to do with that."

"So what is it?"

After a moment of silence, she glanced toward the cashier's desk, where the proprietress was busy toting up her register once again while mumbling mean things.

"I'm in deep shit here as you see me."

"That, for one thing, is easy to see."

"I've lost everything."

"Everything?"

"Yes. All my stuff was stolen in the studio we rent with three other girlfriends. I think they're the ones behind the job."

"What do they have against you?"

"Oh, the usual! It's our own little war between girls, you know."

"My apologies, but I don't understand. What war?"

"I really don't feel like talking about this."

"You're wrong not to trust me. Let yourself go, perhaps God is sending me and…"

"So you believe in God?"

"Of course. I was baptized some…"

"Okay, what do you want me to tell you? It's jealousy. It happens, you know? I'm not from here, I'm from the country over there originally. What's more, I have real clients, whites who come from the center of town to pick me up in their cars, and this kind of stuff, it makes them jealous, my girlfriends. We've been fighting a lot lately, and yesterday, when I came home, my stuff wasn't there, I had money, dollars I got from an American, everything's gone! That's what I was explaining to the proprietress at the cashier's desk. Now while I'm waiting I'm in a hotel, but I'm going to get my revenge, I'm going to prove to them who I am. I haven't crossed the Mayi River in a canoe to let any old nobody bug the shit out of me. I am here because I didn't get the opportunity to do anything other than what I'm doing. I don't have any parents to rely on, so the little I make, I make in this manner. I'm sorry, I shouldn't have told you all that…"

"And the proprietress, I saw she was showing you a notebook and that you…"

"That's something else. We have things together, and she's always screwing me. But it's nothing, this stuff."

"She can hear you, she's looking in our direction…"

"I don't give a damn."

"If you're in deep shit, can I pay your hotel for tonight?"

"No way! I didn't come over for this. I still have my pride, I do. Anyway, that's not how it works!"

"I only want to do it because I want to help you."

"But why?"

"Because I'm like that, I like to help my brethren, without any agenda in mind."

"So you're married?"

"No, why? Do I look like a married man?"

She stared at me. My rectangular head seemed heavier than usual. I read in her gaze that I wasn't handsome. She must have concluded that it was my ugliness that dissuaded women from living under the same roof as I did. Just in time, as she realized I guessed her thoughts, she caught herself.

"You want to help me!"

"Yes, and I'm not kidding."

"Tell me, what man is going to pay a hotel room for a *hostess* and not sleep with her?"

"I sincerely want to help you."

"We might as well go to your place, we do our business, you pay me, and that way I won't look like a beggar."

"Is this how you go about it with everybody, then?"

"No, you look kind and generous. I'm not out to make a profit like the girls from He-Who-Drinks-Water-Is-An-Idiot. Are we going or not?"

I wasn't expecting events to turn in my favor. I was now looking at Germaine as an ideal prey. I wasn't prepared to take a girl home, and none until then had entered this secret garden I had built with my own hands...

I didn't have any car on hand that day. We walked and chatted about everything and nothing, and Germaine was surprised to see how I cut through streets to arrive near the neighborhood's last dwellings quickly.

"Whoa, you sure know this neighborhood well!"

"I was born here and I grew up here. My house is the

one across the street, where you can see the bamboo gate."

I pushed the gate.

"What's that behind these iron sheets?"

"It's my workshop, I do sheet-iron and auto-body work, you want to see?"

"If you want."

We headed toward the shed and I removed the two bricks that hold the workshop's door closed. We went in after I turned on the light.

"My God, what a mess! And you work in here?"

"Well, yes I do!" I said, hiding my irritation, for she was criticizing my place of work, therefore she was criticizing me, and I took this as an insult, which reminded me of the chaos of centuries past.

"How in hell do you manage to work in here?"

"I can find my way around. Here are two cars I've been fixing up lately. I took everything apart. This scrap heap nearby, it's car doors I salvage from the junkyard, they may come in handy. Here is the furnace. Watch out for the grease on the floor. Behind there are other things…"

After the brief visit to my workshop, I led her into the house. I felt as if I were stripping myself naked, allowing a person who was heavy with sins to come soil my holy place.

I turned on the living-room light.

"I built this house myself with my own hands. There are two bedrooms. This one is mine. The other one is in case I'd be hosting friends."

"So you are a mason as well?"

"Let's say I dabble a little in everything."

"Your place is nice! There are no photos! You have relatives, don't you? I mean parents, cousins…"

"It's a long story, I won't bore you with that."

She put her purse on the floor and settled in the sofa bed.

I went into my bedroom for a moment, telling her to help herself to a drink. The fridge was full, I had shopped for groceries the day before. A little bit of everything. Beef, fruit, milk.

I heard the noise of the beer bottle when she opened it. I made the bed quickly, everything was a mess. I hid Angoualima's photos under the mattress. Like many inhabitants, I'd bought them clandestinely. You could see my idol dead on the sand of the wild coast in the middle of a circle...

When I came back into the living room, she had turned on the television and was touching up her makeup with the help of a small mirror.

"I'm going to pay you now," I said, searching my pockets.

We hadn't done anything. She felt offended, her face became somber just like when I saw her in front of the Open Air cashier's desk.

"What's this? Who am I? I'm not taking your money!"

She brought her purse to her knees as if she were about to go.

"You did say that we would do our business, I'd pay you, and we'd be even, no?"

"It was a manner of speaking."

"Really?"

"I don't know how to explain it, but I feel good with you. You're kind, generous and I don't understand why you don't have a woman at home who loves you."

I very nearly answered that at the restaurant she'd thought I wasn't living with a woman because I was ugly.

I sat down by her side, satisfied with how things were unfolding. Then we watched television and, around the middle of the night, when beer was starting to make her delirious to the point where she was laughing like a fool, I showed her where the shower was. She was still talking while I was wishing for silence.

She got up, lurched, laughed like a hyena with an itch, and opened her bag. She had everything inside…

After her shower, she reappeared, more beautiful in silk pajamas. She was more lucid, but still in the grip of her insipid laughter.

It was my turn in the shower.

Inside, her shampoo, Dop With Eggs, gave out a fresh scent. On a shelf near the mirror, she had left her toothbrush, her Diamond Enamel toothpaste, her skin moisturizing lotion and other toiletries that I was discovering for the first time.

Was this a sign that she now felt at home?

I could no longer hear the television.

When I came out of the shower, Germaine was no longer in the living room. I found her in the bedroom, stark naked, lying on her stomach, her behind drawn with a compass reigniting my desire in a fraction of a second. *Tonight,* I told myself, *Germaine is mine, mine alone, as the whites in our town say…*

Everything went really fast. To this day I still can't believe it. Germaine came to my house every day, very late at night. She cooked, tidied up the mess I left in the house. And me, I waited to have my meal with her, even though my eyes were heavy with sleep. She kept on saying that I was a good guy, that she didn't believe in men anymore except for me, that it had been a long time since she'd felt in love that strongly, that she was now attached to me, that even if I wasn't handsome, my humane qualities made me so, that she couldn't accept any money from me, that she thought about me all the time, that I made love well while the others fucked her, blah, blah. blah…

Me, for my part, I wished to tell her to come live with me because it suited me. But you had to be patient. Not precipitate matters. So I waited until it came from her. That she herself decided to come live under my roof. She told me in confidence that she liked flowers, surprises, kind words and all these useless things that allow cretins in suits to go in circles around a young lady instead of simply saying: "What do you say, are we doing it or not?"

In any case, thanks to Germaine I learned that the roses that these cretins in suits give women weren't always pink, that they could be white, red, purple, yellow and who knows what other color. Personally, I don't give a shit about flowers. However, you've got to make sacrifices, pretend, play the game. I faked being moved, smelling the fragrance of the roses. And so, what can I say, I would pick flowers near the "Seine" and when she arrived at night she cooed thank yous, kissed me everywhere like a bitch licking its master…

One day, to my great surprise, Germaine came with a bigger bag than usual and announced that she was going to live with me, that she was going to stop whoring, that she wanted to give me all her love, that she wanted me to cover her with all the flowers that exist on earth. It was moving to see her overexcited in front of the man that I am, a man who since his birth has had to put up with a rectangular head.

Without any humility, on that day I told myself that I was truly handsome and that I hadn't realized it. Germaine talked a lot, as if to justify her decision to settle in my place. Then she sat on the sofa and burst into tears. I came to be by her side. I told her I was delighted with her decision but that, on the other hand, I didn't agree with her stopping her daily work. I launched into my refrain according to which whores, like ambulance drivers, like notaries, like real estate agents, like sheet-iron and auto-body workers paid their taxes, therefore were not engaged in a shameful activity. She was persuaded. She said she would continue her craft as old as the world, but part-time, just to make me happy, and that she would no longer put her clients' *things* in her mouth, which she used to kiss me. And she kissed me. Before we made love, I imagined her as a corpse at my feet. I felt in a state of deep bliss. Germaine was sleeping like a little angel, and me, I was looking at her. Talking to myself, a smile at the corner of my mouth, I told myself I would fatten her up for two weeks, three maximum, so that she'd be in very good health on the day of my deed...

I will assert right now that she ate well at my house during the four weeks of our life together. Good eats, good beer and even desserts she chose herself in the center of town, in the big Printania supermarket...

Another day has dawned.

I do not see time go by anymore. That's how it is. When you have a project, you're surprised by sunsets and sunrises.

Two days I've been going around in circles! Am I ready?

Have I acquired the determination that characterizes a person who accomplishes an important deed? I no longer have a choice. I am face-to-face with myself. I can't go back. Nothing can stop me.

It so happens now that today is December 29. The end of the year is only two days away…

Yes, I know now how she must die. Why look very far? I'm going to cut her up, then boil her in a big pot thanks to my furnace, and go eat certain parts of her body on the Great Master Angoualima's grave. No one's ever done that in our city. This is the gift I am saving up for my idol. I can already see the stupefaction in our city, our entire country and the country over there.

Germaine must thus die before December 31 so I can prepare and diversify my New Year's Eve menus.

I am ready for this deed. It will take place tonight as soon as she comes home…

The Murder

1.

Today, December 29, I am in a state of anxiety. When I move around the living room or the bedroom, objects fall on the floor behind me because I tell myself that nothing can be lying about randomly in the house and everything that's here must have a close relationship with the setting for the deed I am about to commit...

I don't have the strength to work, and what's more all these banged-up vehicles are getting on my nerves. I don't want to do anything, I want to focus, breathe for a long while, and think about the way things are going to unfold here, this very night.

I imagine a car stopping in front of my plot, a door opening and closing, Germaine pushing the bamboo gate, and I hear her footsteps, the noise the key makes when she inserts it in the lock. I imagine she's expecting to find flowers, candles, she's hoping to hear sweet nothings. I imagine she'll want to cook very late, she'll open the fridge to drink several beers, she'll laugh like a hyena with an itch, she'll tell me her stories from the sidewalks of He-Who-Drinks-Water-Is-An-Idiot, she'll bring me news of the old fart with his *thing* breaking down who's the head of a corporation, the wad of bank notes he waves up in the air so she makes him feel good with her mouth, this old executive who pretends girls in Heads-Of-Negroes Street do it better and if that's the way it's going to be he's going to pay half-price.

I imagine Germaine talking to me about clients she calls "this one," and especially about the railroad ticket collector, pot-bellied, with a toothbrush-shaped mustache, hair coming out of his ears, this railroad ticket collector who stinks of sweat, this railroad ticket collector who calls her all kinds of names, this railroad ticket collector who makes her bark like an Alsatian or a bulldog, this railroad ticket collector who comes but doesn't pay, I imagine her telling me that she and her friends jumped on this bastard who fled running, his face marked with scratches, I imagine all this, and then I don't give a shit...

My hands are swelling and they're hurting real bad. A few moments ago, blood came out of my nostrils. That was the first time this happened to me. I think it's because of the anxiety. I brushed my nose lightly with the back of my hand. When I saw blood on my skin, I sort of had a feeling of repulsion, I wanted to throw up. Maybe because it was my own blood. It was a shade of red both heavy and bright. I immediately lay down on the sofa bed for about ten minutes, then got up to wet my face. Inside the shower, I saw myself in the mirror. I'd become old overnight—me, who never really had any age and never wanted anyone to know my age! This is the advantage of ugliness. People say you're ugly, therefore they always think you're older than people of your generation, although that's wrong. Who in this city knew Angoualima's age? No one. And why? Precisely because no one could speculate about his birth date. One day I would like people to ask the same questions about me. For people to know the date of my death, but ignore that of my birth. Germaine tried every trick in the book to find out my age, she gave up. I don't have a birth certificate, I tore it up as a child when I found it among documents belonging to the last family the State placed me with. I don't have any ID, what would it be good for in this city anyway? Nothing, except for registering at city hall in order to vote in the municipal elections. Me, I've never voted. Like Angoualima, I shit on society…

Once my face was washed and the blood gone from my nostrils, I looked at myself again for a moment. My rectangular head nearly filled up the entire mirror. I have trouble recognizing myself. I feel foreign. Is this face the same as that of a few days ago? I'm convinced I have changed. A vein bisects my scalp and vanishes somewhere between the ridges of my brow, which is very prominent, given my small eyes. Usually, this vein only appears when I'm overexcited. I cut my hair with a Bic blade. In fact, and this may be a form of provocation, I like my scalp to be bald as an egg. I know this reveals its macrocephalic shape even more. But I don't give a damn. I could have let my hair grow a little so as to partly mask all this. To what end? Ever since my youth I've been used to putting up with a shaved head. I run my hand over it from time to time, and notice these deep sinuosities, as if God had given me this scalp after some hard labor with a hammer…

I kept on staring at my features, without flinching. Angoualima's face appeared instead of mine. It is for this reason that I refrained from hitting this mirror with my fist to later lick the blood that would be trickling from my veins. I am not going to go after the Great Master, am I? Where are we going? In fact, it is good that my idol is within me, this reassures me, gives me wings and comforts me with the idea that the gesture I am about to perform in a few hours interests him as well…

2.

It's four p.m.

Germaine should be at the Open Air restaurant for her daytime work. I have just stored her large bag in a corner so I can make it disappear in the fetid waters of the "Seine" after the murder. She always takes the smaller of the two bags with her to the Open Air restaurant so she can later move on to the alleys of He-Who-Drinks-Water-Is-An-Idiot at around six p.m.

Before moving the large bag, I searched it out of curiosity. Germaine only opens it when she's got an important and lucrative appointment with whites in the center of town. I discovered an entire arsenal for her nocturnal activity. In no particular order, I saw makeup products, a blond wig, another that was red, another that was plain green, I saw red leather thongs, weird panties with well-designed holes up front to allow women's things to stick out, I saw fluorescent brassieres, bras with holes that left the nipples outside, I saw shoes that instantly made you several inches taller, shoes with pistol-shaped heels, with chair-leg-shaped heels, with isosceles triangle-shaped heels, I saw tights with a pattern showing the man's thing penetrating the woman's thing, pink tights, yellow tights, blood-red tights, tights, that's all there was in her bag, I saw all kinds of perfumes, I opened the bottles, I smelled good ones, bad ones, some that were more or less good, some more or less bad, strong ones, light ones, some that were more or less strong, some more or less light, some that made me sneeze, some that stung my eyes, I smelled all that, I also saw very pointy fake nails that are perhaps used to scratch the backs of clients who ask for it, rainbow-colored nail polishes, transparent ones, glittery ones, I saw a long leather whip with a handle shaped like the two balls of a man's thing, handcuffs, a muzzle, and me who believed muzzles were for dogs, I saw condoms on which it was written that they tasted like strawberry, like peach, like papaya, like kiwi, like plum, I saw a fur coat, but it was probably fake because I know these coats are expensive, or maybe it's a real one, some white might well have given it to her, I saw several varieties of dildos that represented blacks' things and whites' things, I noticed that dildos of blacks' things are bigger than dildos of whites' things even though it's whites who manufacture them themselves, they could have at least taken this opportunity to show us that some whites' things are bigger than blacks', I saw rubber rings to decrease the size of the best endowed man's thing, I saw Vaseline which helps palliate dryness in a woman's thing, I saw other work tools, and I told myself that it was real work this business we took lightly, believing that for these streetwalkers, the whole thing boiled down to opening their legs and receiving the secretion of the male in heat, and I also told myself that the fish in the "Seine" were going to be surprised, the fish who've been complaining that all they do is wade in shit that Left Bankers send them in little baggies.

It's eight p.m.

Time has gone by fast. Some time ago I cleaned a big container in my workshop. It's a type of cauldron that allows me to melt aluminum when my work requires it. I will cook Germaine in it. Scouring that caldron, I caught sight of a hammer hanging from the wall. I thought instantly about notary–real estate agent Fernandes Quiroga's skull. It's a portent. If my eyes landed on this hammer, it's because I must use it tonight. This time around, I will hit the temples, the nape of the neck, the center of the skull, the forehead relentlessly. I will check that Germaine is no longer breathing. And if she's still breathing, I will hit again until the brain is damaged. Afterwards, I will be able to do my work as a cook, as a butcher, like the European criminal Sadilleck…

It's nine p.m.

I got the hammer off the wall in order to take it to the house. Once in the shower, I cleaned it. I didn't look at myself lest I see Angoualima's features materialize. You never know what he's thinking. He is so unpredictable that I expect anything and everything from him. I know that by looking at myself, I am going to notice the metamorphosis of my face again. What use would that be?

I hid the hammer under the sofa-bed, at the spot where I usually sit. At the opportune time, all I'll need to do is slip my hand under to grab the tool by the end I left sticking out. I often settle down right at this spot to watch television. Germaine settles right next to me so she can lean her head against my left shoulder and I can caress her with my right hand. It is this very hand that will grab the hammer…

Oh shit! What am I seeing? Where am I? It's not possible! I dare not believe it! It's already half past midnight and I still haven't heard a car stopping in front of my plot! Usually Germaine arrives around eleven, or half past.

I keep checking my watch and getting anxious every time a car drives down the street. I have already gone out several times to see whether there were gypsy cabs on the horizon that might come down this street. The street is calm, the neighborhood must be sleeping. I waited in front of the gate for a few minutes. Nothing. It's a bit cool. The sky is very dark, streaked by lightning from time to time.

It's going to rain tomorrow. That's for sure…

I think it would be wiser to take a breath, pace up and down the plot.

I get up and glance over to where I've hidden the hammer.

I'm going to go out.

I hear a noise outside.

Germaine is coming.

No, it's a moped. She's not going to be escorted back here by one of her clients on a moped, is she? Who does she think I am? It's an outrage, it is! And what would I look like, huh? An imbecile? A cuckold? Who is he anyway, this moped rider?

I crack the door open, the moped didn't stop. It drove past my plot.

On the one hand I'm reassured, on the other hand I wish it had stopped in front of my plot of land with Germaine on it. At least I could have moved on to more serious matters…

I must calm down. That's it, I must. My place is in the house and not in front of the plot. I have to go back inside, for this upcoming scene I myself have to be the setting. The hour is a bit off. Never mind, my determination is the same…

I am now sitting in the sofa bed.

Sometimes I try to grab the end of the hammer. I don't even see the program that's showing on television.

Everything in the house is tidied up. There are flowers on the table near red candles, which, at this rate, are all going to melt before Germaine arrives.

I move my legs constantly. I check that blood is not coming out of my nostrils. My hands are going to burst. I must calm down. Yes, I must.

So I lie down on the sofa bed and think of something else. My thoughts don't go very far, they come to rest on my idol's shadow. No, I want to think of something else, I said!

Impossible.

I feel the Great Master's hands with their twelve fingers trying to put me to sleep.

No, I must not sleep. I have to stay awake. Is the light in the room going out? What's happening?

I want light!

Ah really, there is light? But shit, I can't see it myself! Wait, I can, I can indeed see it, but it's the stars twinkling, as if my house no longer had a roof!

How marvelous—I can now see the sky from my sofa bed! I must count these stars, one after the other, I must count them, I will get there, one star, two stars, three stars, four stars or five stars, no five stars or four stars, where was I again, the one on the left I counted already, it came back on that side, I won't count it twice, so we were saying five stars, plus this one, that makes six, plus another that makes seven good stars, seven good stars plus one good star that makes how many good stars, eight good stars, of course, and plus this one nearby, that makes nine good stars, I add another good one and end up with ten good stars, and well fuck! Stars, more stars, they're everywhere, they're coming down toward me, I'm going to take another two or three, this one, no that one, no the one that's a bit farther I'll take because it is brighter, it must be the North Star, as the people who watch these things by means of their telescopes say, yes it is indeed the North Star, I'm going to take it, then I am going to put it in a cage so that it lights up my whole living room, I will no longer need the light of day, I won't give a shit about the sun, I will have my own star, well, well, what do I see now, an abyss, an immense, opaque abyss, clouds swirling, swirling again, and me, I feel I am becoming light as a feather, like a minuscule cotton ball, like a fishing line float, I can even fly without wings, too bad for the birds, I feel carried upward by a levitation I can no longer resist, no, I want to come back down, yes I want to come back down, as fast as possible, I'm afraid of falling, I'm afraid to crash on the crest of these mountains I can see below, I must come down, but very slowly, I will get there, what are these distant voices, it's the echo from the television, what is the television doing in the middle of these swirling clouds, and after all I don't give a shit, my eyelids are closing, I do not resist sleep, which just got the better of me, well shit...

3.

The truth is it's the noise from the TV that woke me up just now. Oh shit, I slept on this sofa bed? I didn't shut the door? Maybe Germaine forgot to shut it when she came back very late at night. But no, that's not it.

I don't understand anything anymore. I rub my eyes and look at the time: five in the morning! It's day already, this is how it is at this time of year in our city. The sun rises very early and rushes to set around five or six in the evening...

I have no precise memory of the moment when I let myself be overcome by sleep on this sofa bed. All I know, more or less, is that it was as if I were being rocked by Angoualima's twelve-fingered hands. I felt so good among the stars I was counting. I was like a child. I was able to fly, without wings, and travel over unimaginable distances.

Never had I experienced such deep sleep. As if I'd walked for a long time and, exhausted, needed to regain my strength. I also know that I attempted to resist this sleep, but it was in vain…

I get up and head toward the bedroom.

The bed is made neatly, the way Germaine usually makes it, without a wrinkle, and with the pillowcases set next to each other, almost glued.

So Germaine didn't come back last night. I should have expected it, there are greedy clients, especially in the center of town. But she couldn't do this to me. Did she tell herself that I might worry?

I come back into the living room.

Germaine's big bag, which I had stored in a corner, is still there. From this I infer that I haven't gone and thrown her into the "Seine" as I had planned. If the bag weren't in its place, I would have told myself that I doubtlessly killed Germaine and didn't remember it. I've heard stories like this. Unbelievable but true. Apparently some criminals kill, then feel alienated from their deed and even ask themselves if they are criminals. For them, all this seems distant and foreign. Apparently, others also kill by proxy, sort of. You think they've killed but, in reality, they lent a hand. Stories like this one, I've have heard a few.

It so happens that Germaine's bag hasn't moved. It so happens that my hammer is still under the sofa bed, I can see one end from here. It so happens all the candles from the day before melted and even nearly burned the tablecloth. It so happens the flowers wilted too. It so happens I'm wearing the same clothes but they're not soiled with blood. It so happens the house is nicely tidied up.

It so happens that…

Now what are these people saying on TV?

Tell me that I'm dreaming, that I'm not awake. No, I don't want to believe it. I pinch my cheek, I feel pain, therefore I'm not dreaming.

What are they telling me, these journalists? That a murder did indeed take place around midnight? That the victim is a streetwalker from the country over there? What are they doing now, they're even showing the victim! It's horrible!

I step forward, my nose only a few centimeters from the screen. It is Germaine, indeed it is! Her body is lying in one of the streets of the Right Bank district, Three-Martyrs Street, on the other side of town…

Oh shit, now I'm starting to panic. Now I'm telling myself: What proves I did not leave the house to go kill her in this lane? What proves I wasn't manipulated by a spirit to whom I lent my hand? But it's not possible, I didn't do this! I slept all night, I did!

Now journalists are talking about a surge in major crimes. And now they're embarking on risky parallels, concluding that this surge in crime brings to mind the era of the famous Angoualima. And now they've dug up archival images and are showing them!

I do not leave the screen, I sit on the floor, my heart beating very hard. We're shown black-and-white images, and I once again see my idol's corpse in the middle of a circle on the wild coast sand like in the picture I hide under my bed. And we're reminded of the Great Master's most ignoble crimes.

And after that, we're told about Germaine again.

I try to follow the explanations given by an old lady introduced as the prime witness of this midnight murder in Three-Martyrs Street.

Basically, she saw everything, she saw everything with her own eyes.

"So you are the witness to this murder," the journalist says. "What does one feel after being, as you were, witness to such a barbaric act?"

"It's horrible!"

"We understand your emotion, madame… ."

"I will never forget this night in all my life! It's horrible, I'm telling you!"

"That's for sure, madame…"

"I feel like at every instant I'm seeing this man relentlessly go after this poor girl with a knife."

"Tell us about it, madame. . ."

"Stabbing, more stabbing, I'm telling you! What's more, I'm telling you, the girl, who was staggering along, who could barely scream, who was trying to escape. What's more, I'm telling you, the man was still stabbing, stabbing again, screaming: 'Bitch, I got you in the end, what did you think? That I was not going to kill you one day?'"

"And what were you doing outside, madame? Because after all it was midnight!"

"I had a sort of a dream, I'm telling you!"

"Yes?"

"I'm telling you!"

"And what were you dreaming about?"

"I was dreaming that I had forgotten to take out the garbage. I woke up with a start: and indeed I hadn't taken out the garbage in front of my plot, I'm telling you!"

"And you told yourself that this had to be done at any cost that night?"

"Yes, I'm telling you! I'm a neat freak, I told myself that I had to take it out for the five a.m. pick-up, otherwise the neighborhood dogs would do their grocery shopping in my plot."

"And yet Three-Martyrs Street is one of the calmest in the city!"

"Oh, you know, this riff-raff no longer just kills in He-Who-Drinks-Water-Is-An-Idiot, I'm telling you."

"So the murderer saw you?"

"Yes, I'm telling you, he saw me."

"Explain to us then…"

"The man in question, after stabbing the girl he'd had an argument with, several times, he came near me, I'm telling you. I was scared, I'm telling you! I wasn't moving! Yes, I couldn't move anymore, and you, in my place, would you have been able to move? The man in question bullied me, he showed me his knife reddened with blood and told me that if I didn't call the police, he would kill me too. And me, I'm telling you, I ran into the house like a crazy woman to make that call. When the police came with the television people, the man was near the corpse, insulting it, laughing, peeing on it and repeating: 'I shit on society,' I'm telling you…"

What? Did I hear right? They're claiming that the criminal has even been arrested? That he himself surrendered to the precinct? Therefore it is not me, because I am at home, because I am in front of the television. Personally, I would like to see his face. I would like to see this man's face.

Well fuck, instead of showing us Angoualima's body, instead of showing us Germaine's body, instead of running a loop of this old lady's interview in which she endlessly repeats, "I'm telling you!" show us the face of the man who stole the one who was going to be my corpse!

No? We cannot be shown the murderer? And why not? Presumed innocence?

But what kind of presumed innocence are they talking about? There's a criminal who acknowledges his crime, there's a witness who saw him, saw him with her own eyes, and they're humming their song about presuming innocence, respecting individual freedoms? Do they think this old lady who saw everything, saw everything with her own eyes, can lie? Were they never taught that old people always tell the truth? Where are we going?

And now it's our city's police chief congratulating his men. And now it's the mayor talking, talking some more and always talking.

Okay, so basically they're saying they don't know where the victim lived and that it's no longer important. Therefore they don't give a shit, because as far as they're concerned the investigation is over even before it got under way. This is how it goes here when they've got someone in the bag. They congratulate themselves. They have something to sink their teeth into.

I tell myself that in a normal situation, there would have

been a detective like in the movies or in crime novels. This detective would wear a beige overcoat, a black felt hat and would smoke a pipe, or Gauloises or Gitanes with no filter. He would have gotten over to the crime scene and, with tongs, would have picked up a ring here, an earring there, a lock of hair or a perfume sample a little bit farther on. And the wheels would have started turning. The detective would have first asked himself a fundamental question: *Why Germaine and not another prostitute?* Then another: *What was her schedule before the crime?* Then another one again: *Did she have a dispute with someone in her circle?* Then another one yet again: *Did she have a pimp, a husband, a boyfriend?* Then another one yet again: *Where did she live?*

With this last question, clearly I would be in the line of sight. The detective would show up here with his men to turn the house inside out while showing me a warrant for I don't know what and I don't know from what authority, because it's been a while since I've seen police movies or read that type of novel. They would pepper me with questions. And they would see Germaine's big bag in my home. And they would tell me that I could not possibly ignore what had taken place. I would become suspect number one. And as we know in our city, suspect number one means guilty, therefore I would be guilty, and that's that…

I want to see the face of the man who killed Germaine. Could be I know him, this bastard kill-joy. Since the TV isn't showing him to us, I'm going to take advantage of this to claim this murder in Angoualima's eyes. Yes, I'm going to see the Great Master at the cemetery of The-Dead-Who-Are-Not-Allowed-To-Sleep right away and announce to him that I have finally killed my first whore, that the fruit is now going to rot at the foot of the tree that bore it.

The good news he was waiting for, he will now have it…

4.

I succeeded in starting one of the vehicles piled up in my workshop. I'm driving at breakneck speed and run stop signs without being aware of it. I can see gatherings on either side of the city's intersections. Heated morning debates. The population must be commenting on this great event. The morning papers changed their front pages at the last minute and are promising to run in their next editions a photo of the murderer, the murderer who has already been put in my idol's much-sought-after category.

I drove so fast I got to the cemetery of The-Dead-Who-Are-Not-Allowed-To-Sleep in less than half an hour.

The groundskeepers let me go through like last time, when I came to tell Angoualima about my mishandling of the girl in white's murder. I nearly wrecked a grave while parking. The crows flew off with such speed they must have taken me for a mean ghost, the kind that hasn't accepted its death and exerts itself to harass the living every night. I even left the door open and started running in the acacia lanes to the other end of the cemetery, to the corner reserved for the vermin the country deems the most dangerous.

Before I can even start reciting a prayer, the Great Master Angoualima is already outside his grave, standing, one hand resting on the cross. His facial scars seem even deeper to me.

He is a just a shadow of himself. He blends in with the fog a little.

I have trouble making him out properly, but he is here. This makes me want to get closer even more.

"Do not come one step closer, Rectangular Head! I was waiting for you! I suppose, without making myself laugh, that you must be in heaven?"

"It's done, Great Master."

"Which means?"

"I killed Germaine, a whore from the country over there, it wasn't easy but I succeeded anyway, Great Master. I had concealed from you that I was living with her so that…"

"This is good, and how did you kill her?"

"With a knife, Great Master."

"This is good. And where?"

"In a street in the Right Bank, Great Master."

"This is good. This is good stuff, Rectangular Head. And what's the name of this street where the good news took place?"

"Three-Martyrs, Great Master."

"This is good, I am happy! And at what time did your crime take place then?"

"Midnight, Great Master."

"Now, I would like to ask you an important question: Do you, at this time, see me well, like in past times?"

"Not very well, Great Master. There's this fog that's bothering me a little bit."

"It's not fog, Rectangular Head, it's my Ascension that's beginning."

"Ascension, Great Master? It's marvelous, Great Master!"

"You know what it means for me?"

"No, Great Master, I don't know."

"It means I must reach Heaven for the final judgment. But I have good lawyers, and apparently they've never lost a case up there…"

"This is marvelous, Great Master… !"

"Yes, but I must get there without reproaching myself with the fact that a cretin on earth failed to tell me something…"

"Great Master, in fact…"

"Shut up! Did you turn off the television before coming here?"

"No Great Master, why?"

"Who do you think I am, Rectangular Head?"

"Great Master, I…"

"Silence! You're not the one who killed that girl! You're no more respectable than the scum who wanted to usurp my name and my acts in the old days!"

"Great Master, I would like to make it clear that…"

"What do you think? You think you have enough balls to take someone's life away?"

"Great Master, things have been…"

"I don't want to hear a thing! Didn't I tell you that you were just an imbecile, a cretin, a good-for-nothing?"

"You have told me so, Great Master."

"You think I'm dead, but I still keep an eye on all the crimes in this city! No criminal can raise his hand to strike his victim without the Eternal Angoualima feeling it deep in his grave!"

"Great Master, I had planned everything, but someone beat me to it, I swear to you…"

"Planned everything! And still you're not the one who killed!"

"Great Master, I think I know now that it was your hand that struck. It's wonderful! So you can still kill even after your death and…"

"Silence! Do you really want to piss me off?"

"No, Great Master…"

"What do you think? If I could still strike I would start with you, Rectangular Head!"

"Great Master…"

"You're just a liar, that's your real profession! You thought you

could conceal this one from me? You have lived with this girl for a month for this result!"

"It was a way to…"

"You should have killed as early as the first day she offered to come stay with you! Now I'm going to tell you who killed her, that girl…"

"Great Master…"

"While you were going around in circles at home like a shithead for the entire afternoon, the real criminal came to see me. Yes, he was here, at the same spot as you are. And I am telling you that when I saw him, I felt his determination. He showed me a double-edged knife. He picked up some dirt from my grave and pushed it into his overcoat pocket. What determination! And he left, telling me it would be that night at midnight. Now here at least is a man of his word! He wasn't one to come here often, but he knew what he wanted."

"Great Master, do I know him, this guy?"

"Imbecile, what is your problem? He knew that you were giving shelter to his future victim because he followed this girl and saw her get out of the cab in front of your lot!"

"Great Master, it's one of my neighbors, then?"

"Idiot! Do you even know who lives around you? So don't go putting such hypotheses forward!"

"It was only to find out, Great Master."

"I've told you to stop repeating Great Master like a parrot! You're not my student and don't ever come to see me again, it's over!"

"Great Master…"

"I said it's over! Go! Beat it!"

I'm about to head back, Angoualima lets out a demonic laugh that gives me goosebumps. Darkness has fallen above his grave.

I hear him tell me:

"You have no personality, that's your problem, Rectangular Head! You want to know who stole your murder? Don't look too far, it is indeed this man who preferred surrendering to the police. He's a courageous man who carried out his objective all the way to the end. The whore had told you about him several times, this pot-bellied railroad worker, with a toothbrush-shaped mustache, she said, and who called her all kinds of names, threatened her if she didn't bark like an Alsatian or a bulldog, yes he is indeed the murderer. This guy has never worked for the railroads. He's a chap from the country over there who resented your Germaine for bringing in other girls from over there to be whores over here. You knew nothing about the girl who lived with you, there's your mistake. You thought you were the master of everything. Germaine was not any old girl. She was a fighter. She ran a small prostitution network, and she never told you. She concealed her game by playing the enticer at the Open Air restaurant. That was so she could keep better watch over the girls in her network, with the restaurant proprietress working as an accomplice and keeping an account of the take the whores would bring in every morning. Your Germaine told you that everything had been stolen, her stuff, her money? It's true, but it wasn't her girlfriends who stole everything from her, it was this fake railroad worker, her murderer…"

"Great Master!"

"Now you can decamp and tell yourself one thing: You will never be a criminal. And if you ever become one in spite of everything, I promise you I will resuscitate myself to burn you with hell's flames. Leave this job to others and keep on banging on the bodies of this city's damaged cars like a shithead, that's all you're good for. Even if you come back in front of my grave some day, you will no longer see me appear as I did today, I am now going to rest and keep on shitting on society…"

The Great Master disappeared this time. Forever, I am sure.

I didn't recognize his voice when he uttered his last words. The timbre was muffled, as if someone was using a pillowcase to keep him from breathing. He had to shout to make himself heard...

The fog became thicker and thicker. Thunder rumbled and it's now raining heavily.

I sit down and cry on the grave of my idol, whom I will never see again...